CLEANER

CLEANER

JESS SHANNON

Bedford Square
Publishers

First published in the UK in 2025 by
Bedford Square Publishers Ltd,
London, UK

bedfordsquarepublishers.co.uk
@bedfordsq.publishers

© Jess Shannon, 2025

The right of Jess Shannon to be identified as the author of this work has been asserted in accordance with the Copyright, Designs and Patents Act 1988. All rights reserved. No part of this book may be reproduced, stored in or introduced into a retrieval system, or transmitted, in any form or by any means (electronic, mechanical, photocopying, recording or otherwise) without the written permission of the publishers.

Any person who does any unauthorised act in relation to this publication may be liable to criminal prosecution and civil claims for damages.
A CIP catalogue record for this book is available from the British Library.
This is a work of fiction. Names, characters, places, and incidents either are the product of the author's imagination or are used fictitiously, and any resemblance to actual persons, living or dead, businesses, companies, events or locales is entirely coincidental.

ISBN
978-1-83501-264-2 (Hardback)
978-1-83501-265-9 (eBook)

2 4 6 8 10 9 7 5 3 1

Typeset by Palimpsest Book Production Ltd, Falkirk, Stirlingshire
Printed in Great Britain by CPI Group (UK) Ltd, Croydon CR0 4YY

The manufacturer's authorised representative in the EU for product safety is Easy Access System Europe, Mustamäe tee 50, 10621 Tallinn, Estonia gpsr.requests@easproject.com

For my mom and dad x

'Back then, I still belonged entirely to myself and seemed very comfortable that way. As the eldest child I was much photographed, resulting in a long sequence of metamorphoses. From that moment on it gets worse with every photograph. You can easily see it. In the very next picture I already appear as my parents' ape.'

— Franz Kafka, in a letter to Felice Bauer, 28th November 1912

This story doesn't have a beginning. I just sat on dining-room chairs with my legs swinging like anyone else; grew possessive over junk plastic, shovelled chicken nuggets down my throat at birthday parties and spent enough time gazing quizzically at the sun to grow yearly, like any uniform sapling. I outgrew clothes and shoes faster than my siblings and felt guilty for it, conscious even then that childhood was a wasteful inconstant medium. At school I excelled for want of a peculiar, comfortable love from my parents, proving perhaps that a plant that's desperate to be measured grows more. I equated nurture with expectation. And so, I studied ruthlessly, endlessly, until I found myself in my mid-twenties, crowned with an obscene amount of paper, proving my brain had grown beyond capacity, and with an ungodly amount of student debt. (Shit.) When the last certificate plopped through the letterbox onto a pile of takeaway pizza menus, I was disillusioned with the whole thing, and not much more than nonplussed at the triangular crease in the top left-hand corner from the steady grip of the postman, where, I assume, he had positioned his thumb. The poor choice of font did not upset me, nor, indeed, did the quality of the paper, which was not unlike single-ply toilet roll. Back in my bedroom, stood adrift on the only spot of carpet unobscured by dirty laundry, I thought about hanging this thing up nicely in a frame on the wall — that was what proud people did, of course — but I was deterred by the greyish leak creeping down from the ceiling I had yet to ring my landlord about, out of fear of making unscheduled phone calls. The wall was wrong. I could've texted the landlord, of course, but the wall would still be wrong. The certificate would have to stay in the envelope and be lost under the bed. A bed that was not even mine. (Shit.) I looked upon what I had created here and saw myself stuck inside a vortex of my own messes. My small room seemed to be visibly clouded by the stink of my body and the stink of my superfluous thinking. After spending two months in my bed, I grabbed the nearest jacket

Cleaner

and rushed out onto the street, gasping theatrically for air. The shock of sunlight made my eyes stream with tears. I plugged my earphones in and began walking through this city I had been living in for years but somehow knew nothing about. I did not stop until a man called out to me and I was caught short by the reality of real night-time, when only moments before I'd been transfixed by a great wash of pink over the spire of an old church. I'd been walking for hours, my stomach was gurgling; another day had died right before my eyes. This man who had brought me to my senses cried something not untrue about the state of my body, which I noted down verbatim on my phone, as had become an unorthodox habit of mine. I turned back the way I had come through the wide city streets and reached the door just as the sun rose, crawling into my bed at about 6am. I awoke, damp and groggy, some time after 5pm, only to drink cup of instant coffee after cup of instant coffee, grab my jacket and repeat the whole pointless excursion all over again. I woke, I walked, I lived on deli sandwiches in recyclable paper and I watched each watery sunrise until my lease on the flat ran out some weeks later. My other housemates were long whisked away by beckoning purpose. Alone, I spent a sad afternoon sweeping the carpet in the absence of a vacuum cleaner and depositing bin bags of things I couldn't fit into my suitcase at various charity shops. With my certificates packed neatly in my bag, I trundled home on the train to my parents' house, resigning myself to the fact I'd never get my deposit back. I swapped the city I found for the city I came from. There, I spent a month or so nightwalking through my old childhood haunts (the chip shop where I got slapped once, the library where I discovered reading) and faced my parents' bleary-eyed questions by day, when I'd knock on the front window to be let in at dawn, like some sort of sloping street-cat pushing its luck: *Hold me, feed me, I have never known the joy of attention!* After about a week of this, my limp, doughy parents tentatively suggested I find myself some employment — You could work nights? — which I ignored. I asked them instead what I could do for them, but they were happy, which was a shame. It surprised me. I found myself for the first time intensely jealous of what cannot have been a particularly exciting life. I was the most educated person in the whole family and I could offer them nothing. In fact, I was the taker. As the weeks plodded on by, it couldn't be denied that they were making a heavy loss in permitting my presence in their world again. I was a black hole sitting on the sofa. A sharp increase on the electricity bill. Food was tasteless, water acrid in the knowledge of being nothing more than a clever shit-and-piss-maker. But even this was not true, as I had to ask them how to go about redirecting my mail. Kids these days! Why didn't I know how to do anything? I stood next to my now comically tiny father at the end of a supermarket checkout, minding the trolley that he wouldn't let me push. My toast kept being cut into quarters. In the shower I stared at pin-sized splodges of shampoo in my palm before massaging it guiltily through my hair. I asked: Are you sure there's nothing I can do while I'm here? My mother put down the book she was reading and eyed me properly as I squirmed at the dinner table: You could start with the washing-up. The washing-up? I found myself stood in front of the sink with my sleeves rolled up, glassy-eyed over a pile of clean plates and pots and pans lined neatly on the draining board. The first piece of serenity I'd had in months. It was so simple. It wasn't that I'd never cleaned before, of course not, but somehow the conditions had always been wrong. Cleaning had always been a nuisance because I'd always be thinking about my work too intently to use it for good, to do it with any kind of focus. Perfection was always somewhere else. But now it took nothing to put my brains, as it were, into my hands and think about the art of each movement. So simple, and yet I found myself light-limbed and coiled with energy. Frenzied with inner peace, I emptied the cupboards and drawers of utensils to rewash them with these new hands. When I was happy with my work, I took a clean, pressed tea towel and began to dry and put away, but the cupboards were not right; in fact, they were so wrong as to be edged with grey-black grime. The only right thing to do was empty them fully and dust and polish and shine. To stack the soup tins and pasta packets neatly. To sweep the floor and collect with a dustpan and brush. As dawn broke in through the smeared window, I saw myself reflected in the morning as I wiped it with distilled vinegar in firm, dainty circles. I was a fool. All those hours spent wandering the suburbs on my legs when I

Cleaner

should have been using my hands. When my mother came down the stairs, the line of her mouth curved into a smile when she saw what I had made: Well done, darling. I made us coffee and eggs and toast and burnt a little sandpaper patch on my tongue for my impatience. After I washed up again, I made a start on the dining room and living room. The immediate problem was not dirtiness, as I'd assumed, but bulkiness and clutter. This second phase required the unearthing of my professional eye, much to my shy delight. The solution presented itself in the form of tucking away family photos and moving all furniture notably inwards towards the nucleus of the room. By mid-afternoon the house was entirely changed, and my father was nestled in a plumped-up armchair, huddled over a copy of some book he'd forgotten he owned and was delighted to rediscover. I felt like David Hockney. I spent the afternoon vacuuming in laps around the house and seeking any hidden dust with a damp J-Cloth. Popular hideouts included the tops of wardrobes and the lip of the doorframe. By 9pm I was somewhat delirious and had to be shepherded to bed by my mother, who tucked the covers up to my chin and kissed my forehead for the first time in years. I disintegrated into sleep. The next morning, I woke to the sound of rain battering against the window and my mother bent over the pile of fresh laundry I'd been looking forward to sorting: Sorry, she grinned, I was inspired! In the living room the furniture had migrated back to their unenlightened positions. I gritted my teeth and made for the toothpaste flecks on the bathroom mirror to calm myself. Any relief evaporated upon colliding with my father on his way back from the supermarket, just as I was heading out with a Bag For Life. I was going to do that! I said. Overcome with what appeared to be an irrational fury, I stomped up the stairs to my childhood bedroom and slammed the door with a satisfying bang. Screamed into a pillow. Eventually I conceded there was not very much else to clean or sort in this place (my parents were monklike in their material happiness), but I decided this was no longer a concern. I was an adult. I snapped open my laptop and by noon had created accounts with several promising private cleaning companies. By 3pm I had an offer for an interview at a new art space that had popped up on the High Street. I closed my laptop and wept, stupefied by

Cleaner

the miracle when I considered how many hours and days I had spent trawling for work without success in the field I was supposedly an expert in. How many emails and speculative applications were sent into the void. How guilty I felt for badgering the faculty of my university via email for something, anything, please? Kind regards. The next morning, I got up bright and early, dressed in comfortable neutrals and made my way into town. I found the place easily and knocked on the front glass for the young woman at the desk to let me in — turns out she was the owner, barely in her early twenties. She explained her family owned the premises, that it used to be a hairdresser's but, after that business had folded, they'd been unable to find a replacement. In a surge of inspiration, she'd ripped out all the sinks and mirrors and begun using the space as a shop/studio/gallery. They'd had a lot of interest, particularly from some older members of the community who'd taken to knocking on the window and shaking their heads at the nudes very much on display in the window. What did they expect? It was a nude-art gallery celebrating the female body, of course there was going to be tits in the window. After chatting some more, it turned out we both went to the same university. Oh gosh, what a coincidence! So really, we're just looking for someone to give the place a once-over every morning and evening, help set up tables and chairs, and maybe stick around after the life-drawing class we run on a Thursday evening — the chaise-longue the model lies on requires a steam-clean. What do you think? Sure, I said. And that was that. She showed me to a little stock cupboard full of supplies, blue roll and bottles of this and that, and off I went. I raced around with a little Henry Hoover, wiped down the mini pop-up bar stocked with Sainsbury's prosecco, and even spruced up the faux-leaves and neon lettering in the selfie station. *Love your body!* I was out the back door before mid-morning with a full day's work behind me, just as the first customer began browsing and hounding the owner with a monologue about how much he loves BBW. I was paid cash in hand and used my first wages to buy a coffee and a McDonald's breakfast. Brilliant. No fuss, no faff, no forms, and I took an immense amount of pleasure in holding what I had earned in my hand before nipping to the bank to deposit it. There was an authenticity to the whole endeavour that salved my brain against the stresses of a modern planet, everything important is stored in the ether of the internet, bla bla bla. I walked home not happy exactly, but placated. I managed over the next couple of weeks to pick up similar roles in a local estate agency and a further-education college, but the art gallery was my favourite. I loved chipping dried paint off the lino, I loved swirling sponges round the rims of champagne flutes in the mini-sink, and I loved cleaning the paintbrushes in white spirit and lining them up neatly to dry. And so, I might have continued there, had it not been for the Thursday evening I was working at the studio, when the owner rounded the corner in a panic while I was emptying the bins. She was in a flap; her model had cancelled on her at the last minute and none of her other contacts were available. Lovely, whiny posh girl. What the fuck was she going to do? She looked at me. Later, I found myself holding a glass of prosecco in a champagne flute while the paying guests filed in and set up their pencils and charcoals. All these people were very interesting to me; sharp-suited women, floaty weed-smelling women, a white man with dreadlocks, a horny bumfluff boy starting university soon. I didn't see Isabella at first — she must have been hiding towards the back while I was 'networking' with the owner by the steam-cleaned chaise-longue. Hiiiii, are you the model? I'm the model. Once everyone was sat down, I went into the disabled toilet to get undressed. There were no clothes pegs, so I had to fold my clothes and prop them on the cistern of the toilet. I stashed my jewellery away, donned the blanket given to me and walked out into the middle of the room. There were going to be several timed sessions with different poses. Little five-minute sketches that built up to fifteen-minute sketches that eventually worked up to a fifty-minute drawing. I let go of the blanket and stood very still. The owner made very intense eye-contact with me: So, if you want to lift your arms above your head to start, I'll set the timer. I locked my hands over my head and picked a spot on the wall. Like this? Sure, whatever's comfortable. It was nice to hear the crowd-sound of moving pencils again, an insect-like scratch. It had been a long time since anyone had really seen my body. I hadn't seen it for a while either. I only ever caught the blur in the bathroom mirror or acknowledged the terrain in the shower. Left to its own devices, it had grown and changed of its own accord — reforested. In my peripheral vision I could see all these heads bobbing up and down as they looked at me, looked down to their sketches, and then looked at me again. I closed my eyes and breathed deeply. A cheap speaker in the corner blasted 'Chasing Cars' by Snow Patrol. The owner giggled: Sorry, I clicked a random ambient playlist. Nobody answered her. My upper arms ached. When the timer went off, I was arranged differently, told to stand with my hands by my sides, then the artists were told to switch utensils, and the process began again. I picked a different spot on the wall to 'Somewhere Only We Know' by Keane. In all the rush I'd not had time to switch the heating off and I could feel my cheeks getting very warm. Still, it was better than being too cold. Okay, this time you can only draw with straight lines! Timer buzz. Okay, now this time you're not allowed to lift your pen off the page! Time seemed elasticated; every sketch session felt like an hour in itself, but eventually, I was draped over the chaise-longue for the pièce de résistance. This was the most uncomfortable position

— the novelty had long worn off. My back was twisted and, no matter how I arranged my limbs, something was twinging. Would you mind not moving so much, please? I thought about Kate Winslet in *Titanic*, and predatory Hollywood, and how shit it was to be a body. I might as well have been tired and naked and staring into space on the sofa at home. The timer went off for the last time and everyone clapped. People thanked me very seriously and wished me congratulations. No, thank you, I said. I felt so much more naked having to look at everyone's work while they smiled, childlike behind their sketchbooks, as they waited for my opinion. I was still actually naked, though, and there was an old lady banging on the shop window mouthing that I was a whore, so I made a move towards the bathroom to get my clothes back on. However, any time I made any headway, the next artist would stop me with another glass of prosecco to mansplain how they rendered the texture of my pubic hair. The secret of working with charcoal is that you have to spray the page with hairspray when you're done so that it won't smudge. Thank you, that's a great tip! Forty minutes later I was still stood under those hot lights in a semi-circle of artists determined to put the world to rights. I'd been naked for hours and now I was expected to form a competent opinion on the climate crisis? And Coldplay was playing: your skiiiiiiiin, oh yeah, your skin and bones... No more. I really should put my clothes back on, I said, I'll be back in a moment. I sped away as fast as I could. But in my desperation to get away, I wrenched the handle so violently I broke the lock on the bathroom door, and that's when I burst in on Isabella. Every day I'm thankful she was doing coke and not actually using the toilet. If she had been using the toilet, I know this little path I've trodden would not have been found. I'd have looked away and apologised, blindly grabbed my clothes and left the building immediately, never seeing her again. That eventuality was an insurmountable faux pas, whereas catching her crouched over the toilet seat in this way bound us together in a way that was adhesive and inevitable. It doesn't sound romantic, but it was. It enabled her to say the words: You're not going to tell on me, are you? in a low, gentle voice. (Oh God, those words!) I shook my head and said, I won't tell on you, cataloguing a version of her face, voice, and hair inside a corner of my brain to keep. Not love at first sight, just a picture worth saving. She sniffed a little and arranged another line with what looked like a Boots loyalty card. I knew nothing about drugs then; the small dusting round her nostril was nothing less than planetary, orbital to her features and the promise of something hidden behind them. When she wiped her nose, I wondered how it would've looked under a microscope; such gentle, careless destruction. She stared back at me for a moment and, in a small bolt of confidence, I wondered what she might be thinking, if she thought I was interesting too. Then I remembered I was naked. Do you mind if I get dressed? I asked, pointing to the pile of my clothes still propped on the cistern. She smiled and drooped her head back down while I wrestled painfully with my parachute pants. I saw then that she wasn't snorting directly off the toilet seat as I'd thought, but off a pencil sketch she'd done that night. A sketch of me. When I looked at her again, she shrugged, giggled — it seemed more hygienic, you never know how often these things are cleaned. I nodded, stupefied, resisting the urge to tell her I cleaned the lid of that toilet with my own hands because that was not a normal thing to say. And I must be normal. Isabella smiled again, told me that her name was Isabella, and asked if I wanted a line. Sure. I knelt down. She pushed the page towards me, and I loomed over this image of myself like God, my very own personal God. Pervy autosexual God. My gaze refocused. I didn't love what I saw on the page, but that's what made me like it more. It was only a sketch; she'd missed out my face, half of one of my arms, but somehow caught the tilt in my head and the awkwardness of my posture that I'd always hated in photographs. I was simultaneously flattered and hurt to see so much of myself — enamoured and heartbroken in equal measure. But trailing my nose up the pencil line of my leg and hip was exciting, even if coke proved slightly underwhelming in the way so many glamorised rich-person pursuits are. Cocaine is the new caviar. Or rather, the new avocado; everyone eats avocado. When I sat upright again, Isabella and I laughed together for the first time. Leaned in. All in all, I think that short ten, twelve minutes we spent in that bathroom was the purest time we spent in each other's company; the happiest convergence of our fate-threads or whatever. No awkwardness, no expectations, no mystery. I hadn't met Paul yet, and she didn't know I was too strange to keep jobs and friends. A sorry truth exposed almost immediately when the owner walked in on us fucking against the bathroom wall. Poor girl: OhmygodOhmygod. She slammed the door closed again. For a moment I wondered whether we might as well carry on, but then there was this curt little knock, a clipped voice: have you stopped now? Yes. The owner re-entered, facing her body almost entirely away from us and keeping her gaze fixed firmly on the wall. Ironic. The conversation didn't last long: Can you both leave the premises, please? Isabella: But we're celebrating the female body. Yeah... no. She turned to me: You're fucking fired. And then she left. Isabella was understandably confused: You work here? As we put our clothes back on, I told her, not entirely coherently, that I was the cleaner. That I clean places for a living. Her eyes flashed a little in comprehension. Oh, right. We marched sheepishly across the artist-swarm through what sounded like a heated cultural appropriation debate — ACTUALLY, the Vikings used to — and left through the front door.

Cleaner

It was well past sunset now, and the hot sky had blended into a soothing blue, hugging the corners of the buildings, the curly streetlamp. The shouting grew louder. I realised I'd done my shirt buttons up wrong and quietly re-did them. Through the shop window we watched White Dreadlocks Man pour prosecco over Skinny Charcoal Mansplainer, while the owner looked on in abject apathy. I felt for her then. She looked angelic and sad, eclipsed in canary-yellow lighting; Joan of Arc but with a broomstick for sweeping smashed glass. It was quite a spectacular scene. Witnessing the destruction and the trashing of the place, I was almost glad to be fired. When the fight finally died down and the guests streamed out drunkenly onto the street, drifting over the road on their separate ways, the lights went out: blink. I turned to Isabella: That was weird. She shrugged, placed her hand lightly on my forearm, the crook of my elbow. Can we go back to your place? No... I'm living with my parents at the moment. (Translation: I'm living with my parents for the foreseeable future.) I broke her eye-contact and rubbed the back of my neck, cleared my throat. Maybe we go back to your place? Uhhhh... she mumbled. I'm living with — a zooming motorbike cut her off but I filled in the blank well enough. She had a boyfriend. (Translation: I'm getting revenge on him / I'm experimenting / I'm not the love of your life.) Do you have a car? No. Do you have a car? No. We stared at each other — a foot of distance now between us — and sighed for the lost moment. A fat raindrop wriggled down the back of my neck as the heavens opened above our heads. I was suddenly very cold and very sober. We moved under the shelter of a nearby bus stop and pressed ourselves against the heavy-duty plastic. While observing the downpour, I plotted carefully in my mind the series of events that led to capitalism ruining my sex life. How are you getting home? Bus. The 11? Yeah. Cool, I'll wait with you, I said. She fished her phone out from her back pocket and started scrolling. A soft baby-girl voice: You don't have to wait, I'll be all right. The rain turned to hail. I spoke into her ear over the rumble: Well, I'm not going anywhere in this! What? I'm not going anywhere in this! We stood there for something like five minutes and didn't say a word, no sign of the bus. I slid the rings I'd stashed in my pocket back on my fingers, one by one. Still, nothing further was said. The longer the silence went on, the more upset I became. It's not that I necessarily believed in monogamy or soulmates — and God knows I'd had my fair share of one-night stands with people who'd wanted nothing to do with me afterwards — but I lived with my parents now. I couldn't know the next time I would be touched by someone like this. I felt the death of my youth on that street corner; I'd had her breath in my mouth and now we were in the rain entirely separately? She was watching a Gordon Ramsay compilation video on Facebook. I thought to myself: it doesn't matter who she is, if I don't touch her now, I'll never know intimacy again. I'll spend the next ten years in my childhood bedroom swiping left because there's no breath through a screen. Excuse me, I said. It's raining and I'd like to kiss you. She looked at me, and I was so tired and self-conscious now, but I put my cold hand on her neck and pulled her lips towards mine. Let a little warmth rest inside my belly. Listened to the rain soften and mute and the last trickle of the gutter splash and gurgle down the drain. I pulled away. The electronic bus timetable was saying we were out of time. I removed my hand from where it had drifted along the contour of her shoulder and told her, very directly, that I'd like her number, please. She laughed, the timbre of it reminding me of her long-term, very serious, probably going to Italy in the autumn to have him propose by the Trevi Fountain, boyfriend. It doesn't matter, I said. Unlock your phone, please. For the first time all night she looked nervous, not of me I don't think, but of the possibility of me. My presence in her brain. I slid along the bench to give her some room: It's up to you. We both heard the chug and whine of the bus rounding the corner, but I didn't force it further, only waited quietly. As it pulled into the kerb, she pressed her phone into my hand, and I caught a glimpse of her screen wallpaper; this boyfriend, nondescript, in a white shirt and tie. I didn't have the time to winkle anything interesting out of his face or expression. The last passengers were stepping off the bus and Isabella was tapping her foot impatiently on the pavement. In a divine spark of inspiration, I added myself in her contact list as 'Cleaner' — it's always good to think ahead. I sent myself a text and felt the buzz in my pocket confirming I had a means of reaching her again. Isabella grabbed her phone back and left without so much as a look in my direction. The doors clattered shut behind her and she was driven off, off, away into the night. For a moment I felt like my grandfather in his youth, depositing a woman carefully onto public transport with the promise of maybe taking her out again sometime. There was something old-fashioned about walking alone on the pavement with my hands in my pockets, kicking my boots in shiny puddles. I found myself inexplicably nostalgic for a certain kind of life punctuated by glowy streetlamps and the spin of a hoop skirt. A life that would never apply to me. I meandered through the suburbs in this dream, only to be broken out by the shout of a man from a nearby Ford Focus: Oi baby, where was I going this time of night? Amongst other things. Fortunately, I was close enough to my parents' house to grip my backpack tightly and run, run, run without stopping for breath. I crashed in through the front door sometime after 1am and met with the red-eyed grimace of my father on the landing. Sorry, I said, I got caught up at work. He immediately turned his back on me and shuffled back to bed with a sigh. If only he knew. Sat on my own bed, with the weight of all the thoughts pooling in my head, I let myself fall back onto the pillow as if I were in a film. Looked into the ceiling as if there was a camera there. Damn right I'm at the end of Act One! That's what you call an inciting incident! I picked up my phone from the floor and sent Isabella a text: Hope you got hoe safe x. It wasn't until the next morning I realised I'd mistyped 'home'. She hadn't replied anyway. No matter. It was still only 5am. I launched out of bed and forced myself to pause and admire the sunrise peeking over the anaemic tree in the garden. Today would be an exercise in tempering impatient tendencies, I thought to myself. Practising calmness and neutrality in the face of immovable time was essential; the trick was single-minded action. In the kitchen I stayed with the egg I was boiling. In the bathroom, I stripped out of my pyjamas in front of the mirror; watched the obscuring of my reflection in the steam pluming from the shower before allowing myself to get in. I cleaned the house from top to bottom (sans vacuum because it was before 9am — my mother had made a new rule), but somehow I was still sat on the wall outside work for forty minutes waiting for the caretaker to open up. I had an early shift at the further-education college, which, under the circumstances, I was grateful for. They were always very fussy about recycling, and wading through the bins to rescue clean plastic gave me something to do instead of checking my phone every other second. But that was only the morning. Afternoon was torture. I went home the long way and resolved to walk as slowly as possible. A kindly middle-aged woman actually stopped me in the street because she thought I was delirious, glacial-paced and swaying as I was. Oh no, I'm fine, don't worry — just taking my time! Still no reply from Isabella. I thought it best to keep my afternoon and evening free in case she sprang plans on me at the last minute. What to do? Reading was out of the question. Why don't you paint one of your little pictures? my mother suggested. She didn't know about Isabella — I hadn't told either of my parents, it was still early days after all — she could just sense I was agitated. No, I'm not doing that, I said. In the end I decided to bake a cake. That would be a wholesome, distracting activity, I thought. Children do it, and sifting through trashy, sentimental online recipes that were more like obituaries for diabetes-riddled grandmothers killed loads of time. Eventually I found one I liked (a plain Victoria sponge with a plum jam) but the whole thing was a disaster. I was too jumpy to measure the ingredients with anything close to precision and, when it finally reached the oven, it rose with a large dent in the middle. But this wasn't the problem. The real issue came when I flipped the hot, absorbent cake onto what I thought was a clean chopping board. Unbeknownst to me, my father had been chopping onions and didn't think to clean up after himself. When I went to confront him in the living room, I found both of my parents sitting very seriously on the sofa in BBC *News at Ten* positions and my rage was compounded by the headline that they were planning on opening their home to a Ukrainian refugee. Homes for Ukraine, darling. Where would this person sleep? In the spare room. Do you mean *my* room? Yes, in your old room. But that's my room, I'm still in there! Well, you *have* been away. At university! But that's all finished now though, isn't it? Besides, we didn't think you'd be coming back. Of course I was coming back! Where am I going to sleep? You can sleep on the sofa. What if I don't

Cleaner

want to sleep on the sofa? Well then, you'll have to find somewhere else to go and maybe get a job that pays a bit more money. Oh, thanks, I hadn't thought of that! After my perfectly justifiable tantrum, my parents and I ate onion cake together in silence. Later that night, after sitting through a film none of us enjoyed, my mother asked what was wrong with me. Just like that: What's wrong with you? I ignored her question and asked what her favourite job was before she became a full-time housewife and British Heart Foundation volunteer. She didn't answer me, and my father rolled his eyes behind his newspaper. I stomped off to bed and played online chess with strangers. No reply from Isabella. I slept fitfully and was chased down by thin white strips of onion in my dreams. I woke in tears. Still no reply from Isabella. Unlike the previous morning, I moved about sluggishly and with such reluctance that I was late for work by about fifteen minutes. Isabella wasn't interested in seeing me again, I was sure of it. By mid-morning I was defeated. By noon I had given up all hope. By mid-afternoon I was hit with the worry that perhaps she'd never made it home after all, that she'd died in a ditch somewhere. The idea didn't please me, but it did soothe my ego somewhat. I sat in the local park watching the duckpond, as was the habit of mine when I didn't want to sit in my parents' house. The wobbling reflection of the sky in the water simultaneously chilled and cheered me; when the white clusters of birds would fly low, magnetised by their doubles, only to pull away at the last moment 2pm weekdays were best because it was after the mums and babies had gone home for their afternoon naps, but before the teenagers were let loose from school to romp in noisy, bitchy circles. It was the closest I got to any privacy. Living at home with nosy, well-meaning parents and uncomfortably thin walls had started to take its toll. I thought about finding a secluded hedge a suitable distance from the public footpath to sit in and masturbate. The fantasy was historical — I wasn't wearing my morally dirty Shein shit but rather a rustic linen thing (or possibly hessian?) that was hitched to the knee and stained with the mud of good labour. I obviously would have constructed the outfit myself in the nondescript past and clutched the material in my fist as I lied to my employer about needing to pick berries or something so that

Cleaner

I could be alone in the woods… Wanking under a tree or a hedge back then would have been so holy and authentic, without the concept of an aesthetic. Instinct. Sat on the bench, I let my mind wander to the sound of Isabella in that bathroom. Quack, quack, quack, said the ducks. Still no text, no nothing. I hoped she wasn't dead. That would carry an immense amount of responsibility, my being one of the last people to see her alive and all. My DNA on her skin. Or she was just busy. She was probably at work! That was it. She had some high-powered job with loads of computers and responsibility that left her exhausted and incapable of answering texts or putting her evenings to use. Her own private office where she sat alone, with the door closed and the blinds drawn. It's funny how you get ideas in your head about people. I stared at my phone, willing it to carry her words to me. This couldn't go on. Before I knew what I was doing, I'd dialled, pressed the phone to my ear and was croaking a hello, I'm in the park, how are you? Fine. Are you at work? No. Oh… are you at home? Yes. Can I come over? (…no response. Just breathing. In, out, in, out.) I live with my boyfriend, I told you. Does he work from home? Not always, but — Hire me as your cleaner, I said. Tell him you've hired me as your cleaner and I'll come over right now. I'll do anything you want. In my imagination, those words caught alight and skimmed across the pond. After I hung up, I took the first bus into the city centre, bouncing on my seat like a giddy child and staring dreamily out of the window. Isabella had given me the name of a street I had only ever heard talked of in relation to central, cultural landmarks. How to orient yourself if you were trying to get from so-and-so to bla bla bla. You go through that fancy street with the high-rise flats, that's the best way. Oh, whatsitcalled street, I've heard of there! Did you know they have rooftop gardens? Walking through this place, I was struck by the hybridity, the palimpsest of shiny monochrome and silver metal over pale Georgian-looking buildings. I decided to do some googling. Both Zoopla and Purplebricks claimed any single flat in that complex would go for an easy million. I was suddenly very conscious of my clothing, the ketchup (?) stain on my T-shirt, but it was too late to do anything about that now. I was already outside. It looked even more impressive than it did on Google Maps. As instructed,

Cleaner

I pressed the buzzer next to an engraved name card for a Mr Paul Malone. Her voice: Come in. The lock popped behind the electric door and I pushed inside. I took the stairs up to the flat slowly and stalled for a while in the corridor, picking the fluff from my trousers and checking if my bootlaces were properly tied. The time on my phone read 3:07pm. I rubbed my thumb over the spider-web crack in the top right corner for luck. Seven minutes late. Fashionably. I knocked on the door and, after a moment's scramble, Isabella opened it with a smile. Daylight made her luminescent in the extreme; sunlight sheened over her face, seemed to puddle in her collarbones exposed by a scalloped neckline. I stepped inside, zeroed in on her lips but she pushed me back sharply with the heel of her hand. Knocked me back a few paces. I didn't have time to be upset because all of a sudden this man appeared in the doorway on the far side of the corridor. The serious boyfriend — I recognised him by the plain white shirt, the long pointing tie and the undone top button. He looked even less interesting in person; a man made of protein powder and pale ale on weekends. But I knew even then that I was being overly critical. There was a softness to the corner of his mouth, a pleasing dimple, even if his jaw was dry and salt-crusted in the manner of men who shave too harshly without thinking to moisturise. He had a phone pressed to his ear and a hand propping him up against the doorframe. Isabella pointed at me while mouthing the word 'Cleaner', and I want to say he eyed me up and down with disdain, or at least disinterest, but to my chagrin he smiled politely and offered his hand for me to shake. I was touched in spite of myself, as I always am when men take the initiative for a handshake with no hesitation. I was never trained in the art of it as a girl, the act still feels slightly foreign, a luxury. He gave a firm, professional squeeze: Paul, nice to meet you. Then he turned back into his office and closed the door behind him. We listened for a moment to the muffled, single side of his conversation. Something about gross income and overhead costs. Money words, I thought, as I took in the sheer size of this place for the first time, with all the sparkly light fittings and the height of the ceilings. I'd assumed it'd be some sort of modern open-plan design, but my first impression was of a long corridor with lots of heavy-looking doors with ornamental framing. I wondered which one led to the bedroom. Isabella cleared her throat: Shall we? She pointed to an attractive-looking doorway at the end of the corridor and stalked ahead of me, flinging behind a 'leave your shoes on.' The anticipation was killing me — already I felt slightly sticky with sweat and out of breath. But I wanted to elongate the moment. I wiped my feet carefully on the welcome mat and followed her slowly (oh, so slowly!) along the hardwood flooring, past a series of ugly modern art on the walls, all the way up the corridor and into the grimiest, most expensive kitchen I'd ever seen in my life. The bin was beyond overflowing. The splash-tiles could rival Jackson Pollock. I couldn't even see the countertop through the endless stacks of plates and bowls of old cereal ringed with yellowing milk; the kitchen island alone was covered in wine glasses, kissed with every shade of lipstick. I didn't even want to look down at the floor — I was intensely glad to be wearing shoes. As we stood there together, the reality of the situation began to dawn on me. Isabella smiled at me again, golden woman, in one of those impervious, closed-lipped grins I was already starting to recognise. We host a lot of dinner parties, she said, lots of rowdy guests. She waggled her fingers, ballet-dancer-like, over the general expanse of the destruction. There's cleaning stuff in the cupboard under the sink, and there might be a mop and a bucket in that cupboard there but I'm not too sure. Do you need anything else? I shook my head, resisting the urge to pout. Okay then, I'll be in the other room, shout if you need anything. And then she left without a backward glance. I was unable to move a muscle for a full two minutes, furious and yet significantly aroused. But I had to move. Standing so still for so long had adhered my boots to something nameless and sticky on the floor. I splashed my face with cold water from the tap and tried to stave off my disappointment by manifesting how great I'd feel when this kitchen was clean. My state of pure calm, my high-powered frenzy. I'd be ready to face Isabella then with dignity, to tell her to shut up and take off her clothes. But first: the washing-up. I spent ten minutes dissembling complex kitchen gadgetry, and a further ten scraping gristle and mould into the bin so I could load the dishwasher, only to realise it was broken and leaking foamy grey water

Cleaner

everywhere. Floor first then. After mopping up the mess with gritted teeth, I unloaded the dirty dishes into the sink and set about doing it manually. I ran the hot tap, squeezed too much washing-up liquid and tried to focus entirely on the surface area of each plate, each pot and pan. The sight and smell of such old food began churning my already fluttering stomach. It wasn't like cleaning at home. Strange, alive bits of egg, porridge and soggy meat swam amongst globules of fat floating on the water's surface. But all this was bearable. It was the discovery of a full fish head buried within a pile of roasting trays, eyeballs and all, that sent me over the edge. I vomited loudly into the sink, unable to control myself. This was not sexy. I wiped my eyes and cleaned myself and the sink as best I could. Disposed of the fish. Swept dust and hair from the corners of the room, the windowsill, and made a start on emptying the bins. When the bin bag split, scattering a waterfall of trash all over the mopped floor, I was horrified to see the kitchen almost worse than when I started. Where were my gifts? Where were my powers? If the prospect of some love (ersatz or genuine) had rendered me so very stupid and mortal, I could not allow myself to continue here. My priority now was to finish the job quickly and leave; I would not allow my craft to be cheapened by nothing more than a commonplace, garden-variety infatuation. With resolve, I fanned out a fresh bin bag from the roll in the cupboard and knelt down to pick up the mess. A voice behind me: What's happened here? I froze. Isabella picked her way across the floor in what sounded like a very high pair of heels. Click… click… click. With a significant amount of panic in my chest, I told her I was very, very sorry and would have this all cleaned up within half an hour at the very most. As I moved my hand, I knocked what looked like the jellied remains of a microwave korma over my arm and had to stop myself retching. This doesn't normally happen, I said, normally I'm very professional! I was too ashamed to meet her gaze. Who was I? Crouching in a pile of shit with nothing to show for myself, my skill, my education. Isabella tutted once. This really isn't acceptable, she said, and my heart sank in a way it hadn't since I was at school. What am I going to do with you? The loaded silence was made more awkward by the drip of a tap I mustn't have turned off properly. I couldn't do anything right. My knees were starting to ache, having been pressed so long against the hard kitchen tile, so I made a move to stand. Don't turn around! What? Kneel back the way you were. I lowered back down as she'd found me, on all fours, facing away. Now, Isabella breathed, clean up the mess. I reached for the dustpan and brush I was using. No, I want you to use your hands. You made this mess, and you are going to learn from your mistake. She raked her fingers through my hair, pulling a little. Go on. Entirely flustered now, I began picking with my fingers, piece by piece, as Isabella pawed at my neck, flicked my earlobe. As I stretched forward to grab the handle of a milk carton, she kicked me softly up the bum with her high heels and I yelped. Did I tell you that you could make noise? Be quiet. She kicked me again. You're a terrible cleaner, she said, as I made eye-contact with the fish again — it had been hiding under a frozen chip bag. I burst into tears. Sat back on my ankles. I couldn't even wipe my eyes because my hands were smeared with korma and old yoghurt. I was distraught. Isabella immediately skittered away from me and leaned back against the fridge: What's wrong? Her face was all soft and open in genuine concern, but I couldn't speak. I could only bawl and hold my hands in the air. Do you want a tissue? I nodded. She nipped out and came back with a box of Kleenex. Gingerly, as if she was trying not to spook me, she hooked my arm and pulled me to my feet. Brought me to the sink, where I washed the goop off my hands and wiped my nose. Once my breathing was under control, she asked if I was all right. I told her I was. Right, good, she said. I'm glad. Wordlessly we finished clearing up the mess on the floor and tied everything into heavy-duty bin bags. I set about mopping the floor again with a healthy squeeze of detergent whilst she gave everything a final once-over with anti-bac and Zoflora. The kitchen was unrecognisable from the one I had entered not two hours before. Not just because it was clean and smelling of mandarin and lime; the window was so wide, and the sky was so white and bright through it, it made the place clinical. A TV kitchen. A celebrity with too much Botox gone puffy and droopy around the eyes. I witnessed the sun go in via the light fading on the kitchen counter; in the leaves of a houseplant on the windowsill going from shiny, to matte, to dull.

Cleaner

I scooped up two full bin bags in each hand and Isabella led me back to the front door. The communal bins are around the back of the flat — if you go down to the bottom of the stairs, through the fire exit, it should be on your left. (She hadn't met my gaze yet.) It's the one with the grey lid, not the green one, that's recycling, but I'm sure you know that. Yes, I said. Behind the office door Paul was still talking away to his colleagues, same as before: Ha ha ha, fuck off, Piers, you tiny twat! That's less than a ten per cent increase year over year. Isabella cleared her throat but there was nothing more to say. She undid the latch with those long fingers and held the door open. Thank you for your time, I said, and then I left, taking out the bin bags as per her instructions. On the street things were as calm, if not calmer than how I'd left them, with no traffic and singular vehicles wiping past in near silence. My legs were long gone to jelly. I had to lean against a wall for some minutes to recover before carrying on to the bus stop. The bus did not arrive. A light shower broke above my head as I walked, and in a moment of metatheatrical anxiety, I worried about always associating Isabella with the rain. I made it home some time after sunset, goosepimpled, and with something like memory loss as to how I got there. In the hallway, I leaned forward to take off my shoes and disassociated enough for the blood to rush to my head as I pulled myself upright. I think I fainted, I'm not sure. I came to face-down on the staircase, with my nose squashed against the carpet. It was so very on-brand for my particular genre of personhood, that I should understand too late what Isabella had wanted from me on that kitchen floor. I cursed both Sister Agnes and Sister Michael, the figureheads of my Catholic education. I could've been saved. Some time later — it could've been minutes, it could've been hours — my mother found me on the stairs: Ah, I thought I heard a noise. Come in and tell us about your day. With an ancient and specific weariness, I dusted myself off and presented myself in the living room for inspection. Here I am. The glare and blare of the television upset my unnatural calm somewhat. My parents did not notice the strange state I was in or, if they did, they made no comment. My father directed me to some leftover pasta in the pot on the stove which I ate cold and standing up. I felt altogether too lanky and overgrown beside him. He tried to have a conversation with me about something I was interested in as a child, but I was in no humour to defrost the past. I went to bed and remained there for a week, ringing in sick for both of my remaining jobs and wanting nothing but to blot out the daylight. Showering was impossible; I refused to come downstairs for meals, torturing myself instead with subreddits on 'what to do when your partner is kinkier than you'. Most other helpful websites were blocked by the child-lock on the Wi-Fi, and I ended up throwing my laptop against the wall. I imagined this was the point where one was supposed to call on a close friend for support. On the seventh day my parents dragged me to the park like I was some sort of puppy, for fresh air and exercise: There, now! Isn't that better? We ate Whippy ice-creams from a van blasting 'Greensleeves' and I wondered how I might go about killing myself. Following the events of last week, I had received no further communication from Isabella, other than a text hoping I had got home safe x. I hadn't found the strength to reply, and she hadn't called to check I was still alive like she was supposed to. The cord of our communication seemed well and truly snapped. Having made sense of what had happened, how I'd failed, I resigned myself to the fact there was nothing left to do but move on. And I tried. I went back to work in the college and the estate agency, supplementing my income with a third job at the local leisure centre. The role gave a pleasurable, if decaffeinated, version of my usual high. I spent my Saturdays mopping the poolside and shouting after running children in creepy little verruca socks. But there was something lodged in the bottom of my chest that I couldn't quite chisel out. A rotten kernel of something I couldn't quite put a name to, that manifested itself in the form of gratuitous crying and/or the need to smack myself swiftly across the forehead. Solace was difficult to find. I took up Pilates with my mother in the mornings and cryptic crosswords with my father in the evenings and we didn't speak about anything — they either didn't notice my despair or they respected my privacy too well. I increased my water intake and ate more vegetables. Prompted by my parents, as penance I spent a day relocating childhood relics to the attic to clear my bedroom for the pending Ukrainian. Nothing made any difference. I was being dissolved from the inside out from the desire to see her, met with the need to repress the whole encounter. Unbidden, complex daydreams haunted my day-to-day; endless renditions of that afternoon, some of which involved cleaning, some didn't. Some where I actually invoiced her my daily rate for the work I did, some where I didn't. I obsessed like a director on the outskirts of my memory-cinema, leaving cuttings all over the floor of my hippocampus: Let me see that all again, a little to the left. I spent a lot of time in the park. Something like a month had passed when my brother invited us to the gender-reveal party of his incoming child; a day which would break up the monotony of my pining/self-hatred. He'd successfully managed to avoid introducing any of us to this on-again, off-again girlfriend, so the news came as something of a surprise. Like all good panicking Brits, my parents assumed a blasé front: Nice of you to tell us! Yeah, sorry about that, I've been busy. Clearly! He chuckled down the phone, on edge. You're coming though, right? It's *Pride and Prejudice*-themed. I entered a catatonic state; the prospect of attending such a party filled me with so much dread all other emotion was cancelled out.

My body was a husk, a fleshy prison I was expected to decorate — costuming always set me down the path for a gender-identity crisis. I wandered about the house in a dreamy stagger, knocking bruises into my hips and elbows from table corners and door handles. My mother did not smile again for weeks, only hung gloomily over the sewing machine I had to order for her off Amazon. Explaining the value of a gender-reveal party had left both my parents feeling mystified and disconnected from the world at large. It's all very American, isn't it? my father said, as we pulled up to my brother's house covered top to toe in pink and blue flowers. Turns out she was indeed American, my brother's partner, and from Des Moines, a place we all ummed and ahhed over in pretend recognition. I like to think I'm an Elizabeth Bennet, but he (she pointed to my brother) says I'm such a Lydia, can you believe it? She laughed heartily, circling a gloved hand over her bump. I can't believe we haven't met before this! It's almost like he was trying to hide you guys or something! She had the good grace to not look me up and down again, as she had done upon my entering 'the drawing room'. Anyway, she continued, there's white

Cleaner

soup being served in the kitchen, and the dancing is going to start in the garden at 3pm... you got my email with the steps diagram, right? Since arriving, I had been unable to utter a single word. The place was already very full, and more and more guests seemed to be funnelling in through the door, fanning themselves in the heat, and taking photographs. It amused and confused me to see such hardcore Regency wear against the sparse, tech-heavy decor of my brother's (former) bachelor pad. An abandoned top hat on a monochrome coffee table drew my eye towards his grumpy roommate Steve, stationed unhappily at the Xbox in the corner. Looking around, it suddenly occurred to me that I knew no one here — my other brother lived abroad, so his absence could be excused, but everyone else on our side of the family was suspiciously missing. The air was very hot and close. My brother's grotty rented house was too small to be hosting this thing — it was hardly Blenheim or Chatsworth. I left my parents with the woman from Des Moines and went to go find something to drink. Most of the guests had crammed into the garden. It was immediately clear that all the women were living out their girlhood fantasies while their boyfriends/husbands yanked at starched collars and tried to talk about the football with dignity. Towards the back, a fully garbed string quartet were squashed under a gazebo, beside what appeared to be a large portrait covered in white cloth, propped on top of a small, raised platform. Three women with perfectly coiled hair and white gloves were hissing. I stopped and listened for a while — bitching sounded so much better to strings, so much more elegant. Apparently, the woman from Des Moines was going to name the baby the same thing she was going to name her future baby! She'd stolen the name! She'd had those names picked out since she was in primary school, and now they'd been stolen by an American cow! To be privy to such heterosexual nonsense lit a small flame of comfort inside my breast. This was the freedom in isolation; I could have no affinity with any individual in this place. I could walk invisible among them. My brother caught up with me by the non-alcoholic punch, tapped me on the shoulder: is there a particular reason you came dressed as the vicar? I came as Mr Darcy, actually. He raised his eyebrows. Why have you come dressed as one of the men?

Cleaner

Why are you having a *Pride and Prejudice*-themed gender-reveal party? After lots of bickering, we eventually got over the impasse. He told the story of a man enamoured by the prospect of his child but with little to no idea as to the woman carrying it. The whole thing was her idea — obviously. She's a proper Anglophile. But he promised (with something too much like hope in his voice) that she could be sweet and suitably normal, I just needed to give her a chance. He led me over the patio steps and gestured towards the ominous covered painting: She's had a portrait of the two of us commissioned by this weird artist/party-planning woman, with a prediction, a facial composite, of what the kid's going to look like between us. That's the gender reveal. Don't ask me, I have no idea... but it was bloody expensive, I'll tell you that much. (He rubbed his head.) You could probably do something like that, you know. Make some money. Mum says you're working as a cleaner now, what the hell's that about? Anyway, here's the artist, you can ask her yourself... Isabella! Isabella, this is my sister. She has a Masters in fine art, or history of art or something, but she's struggling to get work. Can you talk to her about your business while I go for a slash? Cheers. He disappeared immediately into the crowd before the breath had even left my body. My first thought was a strange one: that it was unfair she hadn't been forced to dress up like the rest of us. My second, entirely disarming thought was that I was not, in fact, pleased to see her. Hello. Hello. The silence that followed was jolted by the snapping of a violin string, and the music sliding into dissonance without the melody to keep it afloat. I sipped my punch. Isabella took a step closer, put her face nearer mine. Her pupils were dilated. I wondered what would happen if I just kissed her without thinking any more about it. What had gone on last time, what she'd done to me, didn't have to matter, we could just kiss like real people are supposed to do. She whispered: I'm so high right now. She tilted her head, motioned for me to follow. In the bathroom things unfolded much as they had before — except I insisted on disinfecting the toilet seat. When she knelt down, the picture was identical to the time at the gallery, only this time rendered in daylight through the frosted glass of the window — a companion piece perhaps. I knelt opposite her, bowed my head to the line. Resurfaced, bowed, resurfaced, bowed. When the last of the coke disappeared up Isabella's nose, I couldn't decide if I wanted to have sex with her or not. (She was using her ring finger to gather every last molecule into her nostrils, and I was reminded of Georgian ladies with their teacups sticking out their dinky little fingers.) I felt like I was supposed to, that all the air in the room wanted us to have sex. It was the first repetition of action; the liminal space between providence and the birth of a ritual. But this was not déjà vu, I felt entirely removed from the situation. How had it happened last time? Who had moved first, made it so? Why did it feel like there was a choice involved this time round? Maybe it was the drugs, but Isabella did not seem as beautiful to me today — she had all the energy and charisma of a wild rabbit, and she gnawed at her thumb, lost in a different place. After some moments of quiet brainwork, my thoughts ventured in the direction that while sex might not make things better, it wasn't likely to make things worse — especially if I took control this time. The world would not have got where it is today without disconnected people having sex with each other. I floated my hands over her thighs.

May I? Sure, go ahead. She lay back against the floor. I lifted up her skirt, stroked her with my fingers until she was wet, then put my mouth between her legs. I closed my eyes and listened to her breathe, tried to block out the sound of the jig being danced in the garden through the open window, the whining of the woman from Des Moines. No — that way... and a one, two three. No, in CIRCLES! Something seemed to unlock in Isabella. She began speaking to me in short statements, strange spoken-word poetry cried out between sighs: Your brother is having a boy. My painting is awful. They're going to hate it. My life is shit! I wasn't entirely sure whether she was having a panic attack or a good time. Don't stop! A sharp tapping at the door, and my mother's voice asking if everything was all right in there, made for an abrupt finish. Knock, knock, knock — There's a bit of a queue out here... Hello? Moving quickly was essential. First, I washed my hands. Then, it was necessary to pull Isabella up off the floor, sort her out. I considered hiding behind the shower curtain but realised with perfect cocaine clarity it was a much better idea to exit through the window. Without a word or further hesitation, I clambered over the toilet and launched myself out, holding fast to the ledge and gripping the drainpipe between my knees. Thank God I wore trousers. Isabella's peaky face appeared very seriously in the window. My fingers began to slip. I said: Go and answer the door, I'll meet you downstairs. And then I dropped like a stone. The turbulence on the way down the drainpipe shook my jaw and vibrated my whole body in a way I didn't anticipate. I hit the ground with such force I felt myself knocked backwards, landing squarely in a low hedge on the edge of the garden. My gaze was flung skywards as a flock of birds passed overhead, and I was all of a sudden overcome with emotion. Birds! In a crystalline sky! I saw for the first time a planet with tiny flying dinosaurs. Did I live in this place? The urge to paint, a feeling I thought was lost to me, welled in the palms of my hands. My fingers, made hot by friction burn, were even stranger. Spidery, jellyfishy things. Oh God, I was a person! I laughed and laughed at the sky above me, until my father's moony face blotted out the sun. I shrieked a little, and he shrieked back. You frightened me! You frightened me! He held out his hands and heaved me upright. I couldn't remember the last time I touched my father's hands — they felt so different now from how I remembered — and then he let me go. The moment passed. I dusted myself off and plucked the leaves from my jacket, self-consciously wiped my nose. I'm not going to ask, he said. You could ask if you want. Why would I want to ask? The quartet played one final drawn-out note, and the chaotic dancing came to an end with a bow and a curtsy. We joined in with a half-hearted clap from the assembled company — the spectacle of the dance seemed to have distracted from my escape at least. A feat I didn't think possible. A moment of uncanny vision had me blinking up the side of the house in a panic; I couldn't find the window I'd dropped from. There were several windows, and the most likely suspect was still much too high and much too far from the drainpipe to be a serious contender. I had fallen from nowhere. The disorientation was intense. How could this be the vertiginous viewpoint? I suddenly realised the music had stopped and, expecting everyone to be staring at me, whipped my head round in a horror-movie jerk. But everything was normal. My father re-adjusted his powdered wig: I suppose it's time for the gender reveal. A chill seemed to move from underneath my feet and up in a spider-crawl over my back, touching something like bloodlust in the pit of my chest. I pushed my focus back to the matter at hand. My brother and the woman from Des Moines swept their way through the parted crowd and mounted the small rostrum, with Isabella following closely behind. My brain caught up with my body; it was not bloodlust, but an ancestral response to oratory. Of course, gender-reveal parties were in. This was theatre! This was what people did before mobile phones! I wondered at my not seeing it before. The covered canvas fluttered in the breeze like a quivering bride, ready to be unmasked as a traditional beauty. The woman from Des Moines flicked a wine glass in a single chime: Thank you all so much for coming… It's an honour to… It's always been my dream to… I just want to thank my amazing… and to Isabella, our fantastic artist… something for my little family to pass down the generations — She lifted a hand to her belly and spoke at great length about how lost she was growing up, not knowing where she was going or who she was to become, and how the greatest gift she knew she could give her child was a projection of a future self; full of dignity and surrounded by parental love, something for them to look at when in doubt about their place in the universe. I was touched in spite of myself. Isabella, on the other hand, looked like she was about to pass out. The mother-to-be continued: Oh gosh, I promised I wouldn't get emotional… we've been waiting for this day a long time… we can't wait to meet you, bubba… and so, without further ado — My brother did the honours. He pulled down the covering and let it drop to the floor with a heavy thud. The silence was incredible. My first thought was for my brother, whose parental dreams were no doubt influenced by what was before him — such was the power of art. My second thought was for the unborn child, the boy, who would inevitably find this picture in the attic some time after his parents' divorce and the nightmares he'd have of what he was to become — the knife he'd take to slash at it to try to break the curse. Although, in fairness this was the preferable lot. In the scheme of things, it was better for a child to be terrified in the face of a monstrously

Cleaner

ugly future self, as opposed to a monstrously ugly adult horrified at the face of a self they had clearly missed out on. I would say this to Isabella later, that it was better to paint the kid demonic and set the bar low. An impossible face. I wouldn't tell her that the real issue was, in fact, more with her skill level and competency in the medium. Really her painting was shit; an opinion no doubt held by everyone at the party, but one that was likely eclipsed by the portrait of a Kubrick-stare kid in Regency ruffles. Still no one had said anything. Eventually, someone at the back (my mother?) began a sprinkle of applause that eventually bloomed into a lukewarm reception. A pop of blue confetti: It's a boy! My father swore under his breath: Oh fuck, what's going to happen now? We were not the only ones to fear the wrath of the woman from Des Moines — Isabella had shrunk and wisped away like a piece of lit kindling — but on closer inspection it was clear there was no fight in her, just quiet disappointment. A stillness. My brother took over the speaking and thanked everyone for coming, repeated that the party was to continue into the evening if people wanted to stay for another dance. He held up a toast to his son that was met with a recovered cheer. The quartet resumed their playing. My father tried to talk to me again, but I rebuffed him: Not now! I wove through the guests, past my mother's sober face, and dashed into the house after Isabella. Caught her by the front door: Where are you going? I don't know. Can I come? Quickly then. We stole out of the house and onto the street. Ran like criminals and didn't stop till we were out of sight. Not that anyone was chasing us, but rather it would have been odd if we didn't. The need to run was evidently wired in our brains — too many films. We ran until we could run no more, and we rested the same, facing each other, hands on knees. Isabella started laughing hysterically, exposing the very back of her throat. Such earbusting howls took her from standing up to squatting down, to lying flat in a kidney shape on the side of the road. HA HA HA. I thought she would soon exhaust herself but, if anything, the intensity of her convulsions increased. Passers-by began staring and I started to get nervous. Isabella? She was unreachable. I worried very seriously that a person could die from laughing — if I was ever close to witnessing such a thing, it was then — but without warning she stopped and sat against the wall with such ease and control, I was left wondering if she'd faked the whole thing. She rubbed her hands together to warm them and massaged the tension out of her face. Sighed deeply: Oh, I needed that! There was a shininess to her head, something empurpled that I couldn't help but associate with a baby fresh out the womb. She made a grabby motion with her hands, and I obliged, lifting her into my arms. Let's go and get really drunk, she said. After several blokey pubs that didn't take too kindly to my apparel, we ended up in an offbeat speakeasy cocktail bar that not only made me look positively fashionable, but that promised a dancefloor come 9pm. It seemed perfect. We took a spot in the corner of the room away from the bright lighting and ordered nachos and stuffed olives and loaded fries to share via the table-service app. I was in something like bliss for a while. We ate with gusto off our fingertips, muddling our hands between dishes like true intimates. Our drinks we ordered in identical pairs, sampling the menu at random. An espresso martini, whisky sour, a watermelon margarita, an old-fashioned, a white russian, a long slow comfortable screw against the wall later; and the world was fluffy. We spoke of only surface-level things, paddled round the edge but, in doing so, it confirmed a degree of compatibility I'd had some doubts over. It was nice to talk of simple things, simple opinions and simple histories; would you rathers and snog marry kills, what's your favourite colour and are you a cat or a dog person? Archiving trivialities sought to re-web those tentative bonds we'd managed to forge in the gallery. And the drink certainly helped me to put forward my sexiest and most animated self. But trivialities could only get us so far. I was dying to talk to her about what had happened that afternoon at her flat, a need which grew weightier and more difficult to articulate the more drinks I knocked back. But things had begun to sour before I even broached the subject. My hand accidentally brushed against hers during a speech I was making about *The L Word*. She recoiled for a split second before placing it back where it was on the table. Sorry, she mumbled, and our fingers interlocked with a teenage awkwardness that didn't suit her at all. The conversation never quite recovered. I tried to recapture her attention with a number of light-hearted topics, retracing subjects we had already covered to try to find where we had got lost, but to no avail. I even showed her a funny video of a cat because she had claimed vehemently that she was a cat person. Nothing. Her head turned to the window with all the silent pain of an old movie star, and I wanted so badly to find it endearing and not upsetting. I said: You don't have to hold my hand if you don't want to. I know. She stood up and I copied without thinking. I know you know, I was just — I'm going to the bathroom. Shall I—? No, hold our table. I sat down again. Being alone for the first time all day unmoored me in a way I didn't expect. It's a curious thing to have an intermission when living out part of your daydreams. I took to arranging the empty cocktail glasses in order of size, beauty and practicality to distract myself. It would have taken nothing to press my cheek against the table and completely disappear. At some point during our conversation the bar had filled up with bodies turned into inky blue shadows that spiralled round, leaning against nearby walls or picking their way over to the dancefloor. I felt as disorientated as I had in the garden. I was so out of it that, when The Erotica Man tapped me on the shoulder from behind, I screamed a little — I didn't yet know he was The Erotica Man. Sorry, he chuckled, do you mind if I take this? He gestured to the empty chair beside me. No, sure, go ahead. He sat down with a plop, and it took a moment for the misunderstanding to fully register in my brain. It wasn't a comedy misreading so much as a classic, fated brush with another man who was irritation personified at this point in my life. Men are from Mars; women are from Venus, or whatever planet I'm from. I put on my most palatable smile: Sorry, uh, I didn't mean you could sit— He cut me off with a long-winded and overly prepared monologue about it being an overpriced bar, huh? I took in his eyes, his teeth, resigned to the fact he was to take up residence in my head for a long time after this was over. He could have been anywhere between twenty and fifty. A loud jeer and a crash somewhere behind me caught my attention. My mates being pussies, he said, rolling up his shirtsleeve. I turned and they were all there in the same denim jeans and cotton button-up costume, standing and nudging, pretending not to stare from across the room. It had been a while since I'd been caught in the middle of this particular crossfire. He gestured

Cleaner

to them with big open palms and indecipherable mouthing, huge over my shoulder, and they responded identically in turn. The call and response reminded me of ballet; a coded, physical language. I went back to my glass arrangement. Thought about how tired I was. The Erotica Man tapped me again: I really like your friend. Sorry, she's not for sale. (No laugh.) I rephrased: She's got a boyfriend. Ah right. (He nodded knowingly.) Has she actually got a boyfriend or has she just 'got a boyfriend'? She's actually got a boyfriend. Right, yeah, but are you just saying she's got a boyfriend or has she actually — This part of the exchange went on for some minutes, but I'm hardly one to judge someone for fixating. When the waiter passed our table, he ordered pornstars and baby guinnesses. He went on talking; about what I couldn't say, because I was trying to ignore him. I had long mastered the fake-listening expression required for unsolicited (male) conversation. Instead, my attention lingered on the way the disco lights waved over the moon-crater skin of his face, and it was quite beautiful the way it caught his mouth opening and closing. I found myself thinking of the aurora borealis; lost at sea in the face of the incomprehensible. He turned on me with the eyes of a kitten and the aggression of a wrestler: Am I bothering you? The change within me was instantaneous. His self-consciousness made a link between our minds, and I was able to call out to the child beneath his dampened expression: It's okay, you can keep talking, I'm listening. He spoke then with all the slowness and dignity of a priest, bandying his phone and his pint around interchangeably as props for his sermon. I focused on asking him questions: his job was his job, but his job wasn't his passion. He has a little girl with his ex, who he met in secondary school — she's his whole world, you know — and he loves his mum, she raised him well. The more he talked, the more I was taken in. I was not often prone to a moment of sonder, but there was something artless in his speech that made me feel with him. Here was a bloke looking for connection in the oversized world, and where else would he find it but in singular strangers? He should have been driving a cart full of hay or sculpting squares of butter with those huge wooden paddles to fit into a Tolstoy narrative, or a bit part in a Chekhov play. I saw the next forty, fifty years etched into the lines on his face. He was a walking short story — even if his life was profoundly uninteresting. When he asked me what I did, I told him I was an artist instead of a cleaner, which shocked me as well as him. The eyes on this man boggled: No way! I'm actually something of a writer myself. I do a bit of writing, you know, from time to time. I've uh, been working on something from a female perspective, if you fancied having a look? I'd be really interested in your thoughts. I shrugged my shoulders, why not? And met his request with steady drunk enthusiasm, ready to give him my email address. But this man had other ideas. He handed me his phone with the screen covered in writings and:...*he pushed me roughly against the wall. I was instently wet. He put a finger to my lips to shush me and forced my legs apart. He left me waiting suspensefuly while he took his cock out and rubbed it, teazingly in front of me. I'd never seen one before — it was bigger than I ever could have imagined. 'Are you going to be a good girl?' He growled agressively. I nodded and screamed (with plesure) as my virginity broke inside of me. It felt so good as he shattered my body with his ministrations...* I looked up. One glance at his face told me he was entirely serious. Disconcertingly sweet and salacious in equal measure. Am I all right to leave this with you? he asked, gesturing to his phone, or what was on the screen, or both. Password is 1234. It's just, your friend's come back and she's speaking to my friend Jakey-boy over there. And I know what he can be like, so I think I ought to — He marched off. While Isabella did shots and God only knows what else with The Erotica Man and his mates, I corrected the spelling mistakes and, after some thought, left gentle feedback at the bottom concerning his word-choice and general lexicon. After that was done, I waited patiently with all the handbags and coats that somehow ended up being thrust on me by strangers Isabella managed to charm. She whirlpooled all these people around me, men collared with silver chains, and women with bad extensions that would definitely have bullied me on the playground: Oh, my God, thank you so much, you're a saint… oh you're so nice, she's so nice, isn't she? So vintage! Isabella hung on their arms, all smiley and liquid, a true girl's girl. Watching her on the dancefloor left me with a mixture of admiration and envy dredged up directly from my school days. Her face was ever identifiable amidst the homogeneous

Cleaner

glob of arms and heads and legs and asses; she was the brains behind the bacterium after all. At 1am I sent texts to my parents to let them know I was fine and would be home later xx — but was left on read. My phone died around 1:15am. At 1:30am the barman called last orders and Isabella, entirely off her face, waddled back to our table with The Erotica Man and a random moustachioed gentleman in tow. She muttered something largely unintelligible about all of us going back to this guy's place to see his new cockapoo puppy, which I ignored. I'm taking you home, I don't want to hear it, I said. Ohhhh, someone's in trouubleee! A Mexican wave of giggles slapped me in the face. At closing, I took charge of evacuating this vegetative clump onto the street. The bouncer, a great hulking bear of a man, thanked me through a mouth of rotten teeth, clapped me on the back. One worker to another. A fabulous moon hung behind as I shepherded the group towards a nearby taxi rank. The landscape felt altogether too flimsy, as if it would topple flat at any moment. Stranded between the tall buildings, the scene felt vaguely biblical. When we got to the taxi rank, we realised Isabella was missing; I turned around in time to catch the miniature figure of her running down the hill. My legs took off after her of their own accord. Luckily, she was in too much of a state to get very far. I found her spreadeagled on a dusty patch of grass next to an old-fashioned phone booth. Where are the fucking stars? she cried. Wordlessly and with previously untapped strength, I scooped her up in my arms and carried her back to the others. The shock of it quieted her like nothing else. Putting her face so close to mine made her all eyeballs and purple smudges from lack of sleep. She kissed me once on the apple of my cheek and some of her breath landed about my jaw in a flutter. I allowed myself one look and saw that her hair was all pushed up like a dandelion. I carried on walking and set her down around the corner from the others so they wouldn't see. We were met by the last stragglers and no more taxis: There you are! one of them crooned. Find wonderland? Isabella smiled mysteriously, chin in the air, and manic pixie dreamgirled her way into his open arms. They swayed together, cheek to cheek, under the lamppost. She tried several times to stalk off again, but this time I would trail behind like some sort of familiar. It took three people to round her up properly in the end, men who took evident pleasure in wrapping their fingers around her wrists and squashing her between them in a makeshift pen. Let me ouuuuut! The Uber someone ordered for us arrived promptly and, with the help of The Erotica Man, I was able to get her inside with her seatbelt clicked on. You know, he slurred, if you're ever — I slammed the door in his face, and we took off with a lurch. The heavy breeze from the open window cooled the first tears from my eyes — blew them off-course towards my earlobes. All my thoughts and desires had stagnated into a cesspit of miserable confusion. Questions about who I was and where I was to go next threatened on the edge of my consciousness. I centred my breathing as best I could, trying to preserve some dignity. Isabella was lost in the performance of a complex one-act play of her own making, flowering her hands open and closed. Some of it was addressed to me, most of it was addressed to the driver who agreed with everything she was saying. He had a buoyant, honeyed voice: Did you have a good night, girls? Sounds like you had a good night... I must have drifted off because

I awoke with a jump as the car jolted to a stop in the lay-by. My sleep-addled brain placed me for a moment in a parallel reality — the world was how I'd left it but colder, darker. Isabella was still talking but the gaps between words had turned into vocal sinkholes. The Uber driver was silent. After we disembarked, he drove off without a word. I'm sure he had his reasons, but I'll never know what they were. The sonder-feeling hit me all over again and the sky, sensing my swollen emotions, sent down an instant barrage of rain. Isabella smiled at me with her eyes closed, at once all-knowing and knowing nothing. Getting her from the car to the doorstep, and from the doorstep up to the flat took monumental effort — sleepiness made her increasingly pliable but harder to manoeuvre. When I pressed the intercom and explained the situation, Paul buzzed us in without a word. My shoes left watermarks on the carpet in the lobby. I don't know how I got us both all the way up there in one piece, but I did. On the staircase Isabella would scurry ahead to stand and lean over the bannister like a Gothic heroine, greedy-eyed and waiting, I think, for me to beg her not to fall. Paul didn't come down to help like I thought he would, which I took as a sign of anger and disgust more than embarrassment, which was a combination that made me nervous to encounter him again — but my concern proved unfounded. The door swung open before I could knock. This man was entirely different from the suited finance bro I saw before. The brightness of the hallway made me squint. He was wearing a serious smile, barefoot in navy pyjamas. All wiry and loose and beautifully made. A kind of nerdy Hercules. Sorry, I was getting changed. He held out his hand for me to shake: Paul, nice to meet you. Our hands met with a softness that wasn't there the last time, whether that was down to the difference in my status or the time of night I don't know. On the intercom I'd introduced myself as 'Isabella's friend'. A title, I felt, that punched above my weight in some ways, but sold myself short in others. Either way, he didn't remember me as the cleaner. Maybe posh people are like babies and have a lack of object permanence and therefore can't remember the person who scrubbed their filthy kitchen floor. Or maybe it was my outfit. Isabella, who was initially preoccupied knocking the rich knick-knacks and thingamajigs off the hall table, revived a little upon seeing him: Hello, Cuntface. She flopped down onto the carpet and began unlacing her shoes, giving detailed answers to questions no human presence in the room had asked. Paul's face fell into impassivity, the kind of look caught in super-close-ups in police dramas. I put on my girliest voice and told him how very sorry I was for bothering him and waking him up like this, only — a snore broke off wherever I was going with that sentence. Isabella had curled between us and opened her face into a Munch scream. Her head seemed to mutate into the grotesque with every passing second. I turned to Paul: Do you want a hand getting her to bed? Oh no, she won't move from there now. We looked down at her together, our thoughts no doubt making similar shapes. Outside the window, the rain transitioned from a downpour into a full-blown thunderstorm that rattled the blinds. A primal exhaustion overtook me. I really didn't want to walk home in that mess. The snivelling, grublike part of myself wondered if Paul would let me charge my phone so I could order a taxi home, or if he would maybe book me one and let me wait here in the hall for it to arrive so as not to be a burden, and I

Cleaner

would write down his details to bank-transfer him later. Not to be a burden. In the doorway I felt myself on the fault-line between one kind of world and another. It struck me all of a sudden that in order to gain any satisfaction in my life I must become proactive in my speech as well as my body. One look at Paul told me he'd been thinking the same thing, or something like it. I let my mouth hang open for a second before announcing just how very tired I was. Paul tilted his head to the side: Would you like to stay? I stepped over Isabella, followed him down the corridor, and into his bedroom. Her bedroom. My brain was not in a state to properly compute my surroundings. A job for tomorrow, I thought, although I got the initial impression of a space built on Scandinavian principles. Lots of deep blues and distressed wood. Paul rummaged through a chest of drawers and pulled out some grey joggers and a clean white T-shirt that smelled fresh and vaguely botanical. You stay here, it's more comfortable, he said. The bathroom's just over that way, I'll be in the room next to it so shout if you need anything. With a hunch bordering on delusion, I pressed my hand against his upper arm.

My reasons for doing so were hazy even to me. Pencil-line manifestations. But like a ship on a foggy sea, I felt certain all would come into focus soon. Paul clearly felt the same way. Gently, and with all the care you'd give a new-born, he pressed a hand to my shoulder in return. Sleep well. The whisper touched my skin; blew me into another dimension. I dreamt an entire lifetime that first night in their bed, from conception to death. I was a spectator on both a cellular and a universal scale; the sperm meeting the egg refigured in an instant to that meteor responsible for knocking the moon into existence. Out of it grew a girl with enormous hair, which, of course, shrivelled white in the end. She lived a full and boring life and died not on a normal bed, but in some sort of sci-fi tube suspended within a metallurgical orb, bobbing like mercury. What wasn't clear was whether the child in question was a vision of a child to come or a version of myself past and future. The morning light coaxed me out of sleep gradually and then all at once. For the first time in what might have been years, I woke happy and without a guilty conscience. The kind of forgiveness you can only allow yourself whilst staying in someone else's bed but without sleeping with them. A holiday. I gave myself a fifteen-minute or so lie-in, warm under the duvet, to leach as much out of the experience as I could. My peace came to an end with a familiar-unfamiliar iPhone alarm bleeping from within the pile of my clothes on the floor. I reached out a hand and out of the breeches tumbled a surprise. The Erotica Man — I never gave him his phone back. Holding this sleek dirty thing in my hand in the daylight made me cringe like nothing else: I had to squint to read it properly as it was more cracked even than my phone and the brightness was dimmed in battery-saving mode. The lock-screen was covered in endless message previews from a 'Laura Fucking Bitchface': *Ok whatever lmk what time you'll be here... I hope you're bringing your own food tonight because I'm not paying for... What time you think you'll get here I wanna give her her bath before the... Where the fuck are you? She's asking and I can't... You PROMISED to come tonight and see her, Idc if you... I hate you so much. I really do I hate... I've put her to bed now so if you were thinking of... You're a waste of a person. A fucking...* Reading his message previews felt rude. I thought about unlocking the phone (what a stupid password: 1234) and contacting Laura Fucking Bitchface but recoiled instantly at the interaction. It was too much when I wanted to enjoy being where I was. I set the phone down on the bedside table with the intention of sorting it later and steeled myself to enter the newly installed update on my life. Isabella was no longer coiled by the shoe rack. Nor was she in the kitchen. I drank posh coffee and ate vegan breakfast burritos with Paul. He made them out of tofu seasoned with sulphuric black salt to give it that 'eggy' flavour. He was a fountain of information, a virtuosic teller of tales. Corporate life sounded good when mixed with boys' club anecdotes in his mouth. I don't think I thought about Isabella for hours. She must have heard us, we were laughing pretty loudly, but she didn't make her appearance until later that evening, emerging clean and twitchy from her art studio. If she was surprised to see me with Paul, she didn't show it. Lady Di. There wasn't much to see at that point apart from us sitting, knees touching, on the sofa, but I suppose it was enough to draw a conclusion. She looked down on us from the doorway all righteous and regal, and I realised I was trapped within a microcosm of bisexual panic.

Cleaner

I wanted both of them at the same time. I wanted both of them in bed. I wanted Isabella and me to spoon Paul from either side under the covers and this man to glue us together in his house. I looked up at her and tried to transmit this mental picture; *don't you see? I'm not stealing him, I'm just joining in on your project.* But Isabella kept her distance, which I was simultaneously grateful for and ashamed of. In fact, I only saw her one more time before she disappeared. Paul and I had returned from our visit to the local butterfly farm a few days later to find her munching toast at the breakfast bar, her planetary nose white as snow. I hadn't been home yet, so I was wearing one of her dresses. We didn't talk much, just exchanged pleasantries. I showed her the postcards I'd bought at the giftshop, and she held them carefully by the edges, touching as little as possible. I recounted some things I remembered the guide had said about the life cycle of a caterpillar, metamorphosis, and did you know that butterflies taste with their feet? All of us sat together and drank coffee out of bowl-shaped mugs. Paul asked her how her painting was going, and she said it was going well. I hadn't been inside her studio yet. I wasn't sure if I was allowed — the door had always been locked, and I understood that the key was always on her person. Isabella was funny like that, Paul said. The conversation petered out, but it didn't feel strange or unnatural, the three of us sat there. Paul and I couldn't have known. After downing the dregs of her coffee, she smiled, grabbed her bag and said: I'm off! Disappearing down the hall and out the front door. That was that — she was gone. The mundanity of it was disconcerting. We didn't notice. Paul was ordering us Korean food, her favourite apparently, and thought she might like to share. He said: I wonder where Isabella's got to? slapping the arm of the sofa and standing up with purpose. I looked up at him slowly, angled my head. Isabella. I wanted the lightbulb to flicker, or the door to swing of its own accord, but it didn't. I'd been staying in her home. How could I have lost her? We wandered around the flat; Paul taking the lead with me knitted to his elbow in what can only be described as a ghost-walk. The corridor seemed forest-like with the darkness painted onto the walls — I was drunk — before my brain bungeed my vision back to rights. We tiptoed along the floor for no logical reason and a hole in one of my (Paul's) socks froze a cold circle on the sole of my foot with every step. We searched: she wasn't in the bedroom or the spare room, she wasn't in the bathroom or the kitchen, the door to her studio was locked when I rattled the handle in my fist. Paul rapped on the wood lightly with his knuckles and we waited, listening... but there was no answer. Hellooo? He shrugged and turned back towards the living room. I grew uncharacteristically high-pitched: What if she's in there and not—? She'll turn up tomorrow. He patted me gently on the head. Do you like Tteokbokki? We returned to the living room. While Paul ordered dinner, I rang her number three times, letting it ring for twenty times each time, but she didn't pick up. I followed that with a disgusting slew of messages, all unread. Slightly breathless, I reclined on the sofa and licked the dried purple droplets on the rim of my wine glass for something to do. Despite my best intentions, over the course of the evening I passed from concern to anxiety, and from anxiety to blind panic. I became convinced she'd overco-cained and was in cardiac arrest, locked in her studio. Paul grew increasingly irritated with me, gochujang-stained about the mouth, but said nothing. It was still too early for us to fight, even if I was being an anxious sad-girl. He went down on me after dinner, which helped a little, but then I started thinking about cats and had to ask him to stop. That night I did not sleep but spent the hours imagining her body contorted on the floor of the studio next to us. The more I thought upon it, the more I was convinced I could see her through the wall. Her crumpled, face-down shape; the way her arm landed in a perfect right-angle. I was entirely certain that she'd returned the day we visited the butterfly farm. She must have. I heard her key in the door, heard her footfall, heard her flush the toilet, heard her swear while she kicked off her shoes. Even if I could be persuaded that it wasn't her, something moved through the flat that was not me or Paul. I was convinced, in the same way, as I sat in her bed, I was convinced something was dead behind that bedroom wall. Paul's total lack of concern did nothing to comfort me, even if the starved, wimpy voice of reason in my ear dictated that if he wasn't worried, then I didn't need to be. I felt a sudden rush of wifely resentment as he lay beside me,

Cleaner

open-mouthed in sleep, the shadow of his fist curled over his bare chest like a small animal. It is not a minor curse that my brain looks for impossible jobs: the more I looked at him, the more I thought he was dead too. Two dead bodies to manage. I had to hover my pinkie finger over his nostril at regular intervals during the night to check he was still breathing. Sleep must've found me eventually because I woke to the sound of whistling birds and the hiss of an aerosol deodorant. I burst into the bathroom; Paul was having a moment of quiet reflection, poking at his own bicep. He yelped self-consciously: What is it? I shook my head, slammed the door and roamed the place, hoping to see her bedraggled on the sofa or snoring on the kitchen floor — but she was not there. The studio door was still locked. Instead of catching up on lost sleep, I paced the corridor up and down and started ringing her number again, even though the person I was trying to reach was not accepting calls at this time. Paul observed all this quietly over his no-bits orange juice. I looked at him: What? Once he was shut in his office, I pressed my belly to the floor to look in the gap under the door of the studio. There wasn't much to see. No shadow, no shape to cling to. The floor felt grainy pressed against my cheek. I didn't want to use the vacuum in case Paul was on the phone to New York or something, so I swept the whole corridor with a raggedy dustpan and brush. Took the rug from the hallway and beat it over the balcony like a good pre-electricity household bitch. I changed out of my (Paul's) sweaty pyjamas and put a load of washing on. Stripped the bed and negotiated with new sheets and covers. When Paul emerged just after midday, we ate fake-tuna sandwiches fashioned out of mushed-up chickpeas and strips of nori. He tried to talk to me about crypto, but I wasn't in the mood to pretend. If she's not back in half an hour I'm battering down the studio door, I informed him. Paul swallowed: She's probably just gone home to her parents. She has parents? Yeah, she has parents. Where do they live? Eastbourne. Oh, right. I collected our plates and dumped them in the sink, splashed the tap. I'm going to Tesco; do you want anything? Paul shook his head, shrank back into his office. With abstract purpose, I grabbed a fancy tote bag from the cupboard and strode out of the flat, down the stairs and onto the street. The world was

Cleaner

a foggy grey, needled only by the invitation of a green traffic light. Faces on the street kaleidoscoped ahead as I hovered on the edge of delirium for some minutes. I was a confident, capable person, who could do whatever I put my mind to. If I left for the station now, I could be in Eastbourne by — I walked headlong into a lamppost with cartoon twang, a steel-pan rumble. The blow to my face, while painful, brought me back to my senses at least. This was a blessing and a curse: a sweat-patched man on his way back from the gym laughed at me so gently, that the shame froze me to the concrete for a while. He didn't ask if I was all right but took the time to look back at me as he walked away... twice, smiling intently both times. By the time I got to the shop I'd replayed the incident in my mind enough times to spiral into a deep mortification. I didn't really want to buy anything, but I played a game where every ten steps I picked up a random item without looking, to surprise myself later at the till. Paul had given me his card, so I didn't need to look at the prices. Back at the flat, I packed away punnets of strawberries, tins of fish, vegetarian Scotch eggs and a rogue pregnancy test that I squirrelled away in the bathroom cupboard. I occupied the late afternoon chiselling out the dirt between the tiles on the kitchen floor with an old screwdriver. Each wriggle of excavated grime became alive and wormlike, travelling to the bottom of the bin to descend into the abyss of hell. With the floor mopped and gleaming, I concocted a dinner of leek, kale and sweet potato in tahini dressing, with torn pittas soaked in olive oil and roasted in the oven. When all that was done, I went into the corridor and took a running jump at kicking the studio door down. The lock broke on the first go and the door swung open so fast, it hit the wall and snapped itself closed again with a slam. I was licked by a spectral, ungodly gust of air. Silence. I waited for Paul to emerge from the office and say something but he didn't come. My hands shook as I reached for the handle, as I pushed my way inside. The first thing I noticed was that there was no corpse on the floor. Oddly disappointing. The relief after so many hours of turmoil was sticky in my belly: raw, half-baked. The contents of the room were no longer interesting to me. I turned and shut the door; scurried back to the kitchen to chop and dress an overcomplicated salad.

Cleaner

Paul emerged from his office on schedule at 6:30pm, tired and sort of ugly: What happened to your face? I probed my forehead: I had unwittingly sprouted a perfect pink egg in the centre, courtesy of the streetlamp. I inspected the damage in the mirror and the smile of Sweat-Patch Man scythed its way back inside my head, unwelcome. As I hunted down something cold to take down the swelling, Paul folded into himself on the sofa and watched Brian Cox on the telly with his head lolling to forge a double chin. I lorded over the kitchen counter, ethereal. The dinner I made was edible, therefore it was a success. After I loaded the (now repaired) dishwasher, I joined Paul in the living room and vaguely rubbed his erection during a fascinating segment on Pluto. At 9:45pm we had penis-in-vagina sex. At 10pm I drank a pint of ice-cold water from the fancy dispenser in the American-style double-doored fridge-freezer. Paul was already asleep when I got into bed next to him. Yesterday's wifely resentment seemed to have been replaced by something neutral and unidentifiable in the cavern of my chest. Sleep refused me. At 2:45am I returned to the studio, taking care to open the door with caution. There was no body on the floor, no body hidden in the cupboard, no body under the desk — and other than a blank piece of paper pinned to the easel; there was no other art. What had she left me? Most of the fancy paints were unopened, the brushes felt too soft against my fingertips. I sifted through all the paper and materials, clawed my hand over each shelf, but no. Blank. No writing, no scribbling, no nothing. I stood in the window and whispered her name against the glass. Bitch. It was the witching hour; she was supposed to emerge. I scoured the street below for signs of life, but nothing moved. There were no cars or taxis, and the trees were judgmentally still, with passive-aggressive branches that seemed turned into arms, turned into upturned hands. I was about to give up when something nebulous tempted me back to the blank page on the easel. Furious, I flipped the paper over and was confronted with the image of my own tits. Exhilaration. Looking my nipples in the eye, I wept hot, quick tears. Her sketch from the gallery was better than I remembered — and worse. I was as she'd left me; with pencilled-in hips and a missing face. Hating myself for it but doing it anyway, I took out my phone and snapped a few pictures of her drawing of me. As I expected, the headless paper me became flat and sexy inside my iPhone gallery. There is nothing more dead than a photograph of art. It *captures*. Isabella was gone. I stood for a long time before crawling back into bed next to snoring Paul, resolving to solve the mystery tomorrow. However, when morning arrived, I was weighed down with an indomitable lethargy that made me unable to leave her bed. Paul spent the day leaving offerings of Lemsip and gently sliced fruit at regular intervals that mostly went untouched. I did not rise until that evening, when he had relaxed into a floppy, post-handjob sleep. Midnight patrols became standard practice. I became spirit-like, a reverse Cathy Earnshaw. Gradually I morphed from a daytime creature into a night-time hag, sleeping into the early afternoon, fucking Paul in the evening, occupying the studio at night. Sunset one night, my thoughts inexplicably turned to blood, engendering the first artistic frenzy I'd had since graduation. Insatiable, I drew bodies stacked in Jenga piles on Paul's special printer paper, harvested blood from my period in a beaker and painted bodily wounds, hearts, organs, orifices. Madly, I even covered the wall with pale red handprints like the Cueva de las Manos. Paul didn't suspect a thing — the rage and derangement was localised to the studio and only lasted for a week. Then the follicular phase levelled me out again. During the comedown, my head deigned to empty itself of any complex thought, obsessing over other people's sob stories in *DIY SOS* and *The Repair Shop* and how pretty I looked in the mirror. My parents eventually contacted me, possibly at the beginning of my second week living with Paul to formally enquire about my whereabouts. Hellooo? Their voices were suspiciously peppy down the phone. I summed up my new situation loosely and cautiously. Nice of you to tell us! Sorry, I've been busy. Clearly! This was soon followed by a request to 'see me' (check for bruises/admire my new gimp mask) and meet my 'new friend' (pimp/sugar-daddy/future husband). Despite the inevitable feelings of humiliation at having to say I was in a relationship of some description, my ego was bolstered by the prospect of introducing someone vaguely normal to my mother and father. Someone proper and filmic and hard to criticise. At my suggestion we arranged to meet at a fancy restaurant-bar in the city centre for

Cleaner

what I termed 'a casual brunch'. Paul had mentioned eating eggs there once (before he was an intuitive plant-based eater) but his face betrayed nothing when I informed him of our plans. He was characteristically resolute, his gaze fixed on the television. It was decided. All week I practised imaginary conversations in the bathroom mirror. I was the curator of the scene, of course, but it became clear from my mirror projections that I should take on a supporting role. Be the facilitator. According to wikiHow, I was a recontextualised person ascending in status, the daughter figure potentially being wifed off — this was about Paul and my parents getting to know each other and me being the treasured thing in common. Both parties would need to lie, would want to lie, and were going to lie about how calm and eligible I was in order for this to work out. Paul was going to ask my parents what I was like as a child and my parents were going to smile and offer non-humiliating anecdotes dripping in nostalgia. My parents were going to ask how we met, and Paul was going to smirk at me, clutch at my knee under the table and say: '*We met through a friend.*' The morning of, I startled out of a dream where I starred as a naval officer in charge of deep-cleaning a submarine. A surprisingly empathetic venture — the psychosomatic pressure was so intense around my sinuses I had to pop my ears. After a meticulous shower I dressed in a skin-tight thing with geometric cut-outs that I found in the wardrobe. Paul awoke bleary-eyed ten minutes before we needed to leave and donned a navy-blue jumper. Reliable. When we stepped out into the morning together, clear and bright, we could have been in New York — but we were not. As we walked through the city together, past the chanting football people and the other weekend wanderers, I relished the paradoxical sensation of being looked at while being left alone. The walk was longer than I anticipated and, by the time we arrived, the high heels I'd put on were rubbing blisters into my heels. The restaurant-bar we'd booked was in a small courtyard off the main street overlooking the canal. There weren't many people about, and the people that were about were unexpectedly quiet. Paul pointed out where we were headed: a bar devoid of any other customers, the most silent and depressing of them all. Ah, there it is! In my distraction, I strode over a curious patch of claggy white dust a few

Cleaner

metres before the entrance. When I stopped and looked closer, I saw it was clotted with an unpleasant black-brown substance. Luckily, I didn't get anything on my (Isabella's) fancy high heels, but it was close, and we weren't the only people treading through this mysterious shit unawares. A stray thought, unbidden: if I worked at this establishment, that paving slab would have been gleaming. Paul stared down at me quizzically and I wondered whether or not I should say something about it. The gunk on the floor by the entrance was really not very good at all. However, I did not feel so Karenish as to want to tell someone how to do their job. I considered all possible angles so immediately and fully that I felt my mind cleaved in two by reason. In the end I decided to say something. After all, I was a customer, a person; I deserved to take up space in the world and make the world suit me. When the waiter arrived — a tattooed teenager with more face piercings than face — I pointed it out and asked her, I said: Excuse me, I wonder if someone could clean up this weird, gross stuff on the floor, I nearly got it on my shoe, and they're quite expensive, thanks so much, sorry to be a pain. I smiled. However, the waiter stared back at me with such emptiness that my throat immediately closed up. She explained that while she was extremely sorry about my shoes, unfortunately, there'd been a murder the night before. One of their customers had been jumped on by a gang of men after defending his partner in an altercation. It's all over social media. If you look up there on the balcony (she said, as we looked) you can see the homicide detective and his assistant. The crime-scene investigators were here up until this morning — they've literally only just taken their tent down and the white stuff on the pavement is the chalk they left to soak up all the blood. As you can imagine, a lot of the staff who witnessed the attack, including herself, are quite upset. But yeah, sorry about your shoes, she reiterated. Have you made a booking? She showed us to our table under a leafy spangled canopy and we sat down without a word. The seats were slightly damp, and the border hedge to our right definitely had traces of vomit in it from the night before. Paul turned to me: Do you want to say something about that? I shook my head. Instead of talking, we watched the homicide detective on the neighbouring balcony above us drink his Costa coffee and brood. When his assistant showed him something on his phone, he laughed heartily, and returned to his brooding again. When I couldn't resist it any longer, I redirected my gaze back to the chalk patch. It was a mottled stain, like all the other mottled stains on the pavement. It was nothing. People glided past in ignorance, the detective knocked his coffee cup over, and the dregs sprayed over the square. Why hadn't they cleaned it? A voice behind us: I had to gather all the security footage for the police afterwards. I was standing right here when it happened, right where I am now. Fifteen guys jumping on the one. Only took a minute or so, the stabbing. There wasn't much sound, to be fair, just their footsteps moving around each other. The man himself didn't even make that much noise when they did what they did to him; he just fell down and died and then the rest all ran away... The gothy waiter left a dramatic pause and then handed us our menus, informing us of the specials. She spoke with a gentleness at odds with her bony, metallic features. I was caught by the universe of silver plotted over her earlobes. After she took our drinks orders, she sloped off back into the restaurant but I could still see her through the trendy window wall, stood statuesque behind the bar. My parents were no less than twenty-five minutes late. Sorry, darling, we got lost; my mother kissed me dryly on the cheek. My father stood beside her and looked awkward. Well, this is nice! she said. Very quiet! They sat down and three pairs of eyeballs swivelled in my direction. Aren't you going to introduce us? I opened my mouth to facilitate, but nothing came out. Then Gothy appeared at my arm and punished me with silent patience. My father spoke for the first time: Are you normally this quiet on the weekend? Gothy smiled, explained about the murder the previous night. Mercifully, she didn't tell them about the chalk. Oh, right. Gosh. With little to no hesitation, my parents searched up the news story on their weird off-brand smartphones. Here he is! My mother held up a flash of his profile picture, apparently having found him on Facebook. He doesn't look fifty, does he? She tried to shove the picture under my nose but I turned away, I didn't want to see his face. Paul and my father mumbled in agreement. Gothy nodded enthusiastically. He didn't look fifty. After Gothy took our orders (Eggs Benedict, Eggs Florentine, Eggs

Cleaner

Royale, avocado on toast), I managed with great difficulty to pronounce my parents' names so Paul could shake both of their hands awkwardly over the table. The introduction was made. Paul explained who he was and what he did in the world succinctly and respectfully, while I watched some stray police tape flutter in the distance. An underripe, stumbling conversation followed: I could read my mother's surprise and my father's indifference to Paul's handsomeness, and both of their responses enraged me. My mother eventually turned her attention to me: So, what's new? Apart from — she gestured a hand at the table and the fact that we, this combination of people were sitting at it. Not much, I said. My mother was undeterred: Well, your father's bought a rowing machine and the frogs in the garden have started to spawn. No Ukrainian yet, she's still holed up in Odessa (ugly pause). Out of duty, I asked about my brother and the woman from Des Moines. She was expanding on schedule. Names-wise, she and my brother were apparently torn between 'Bennet' and 'Firth' for this boy-child. Once my mother began to rave about the party and the terrible gender-reveal portrait painted by the weird hawkish woman who ran off with the money after scamming them so terribly, I fought to change the subject. It was unclear from Paul's expression how much he knew. Despite these initial fumblings, we were saved by the murder, which proved itself more than enough conversational nourishment. There's nothing quite like other people's problems. We were able to talk at length at first about how awful it was, then how awful it must be for the family (particularly his partner, who posted a lengthy essay on Facebook detailing her grief, which we were able to dissect in full) before rounding off with how awful it must have been for the staff who were trying to do their job and close up for the night. Gothy reappeared with eggs on cue, set down the plates. My father enlarged his voice: It must have been so awful for you and everyone working here when it happened, such a horrible thing to witness. Are you all right? Gothy nodded serenely: I already had a therapist anyway, so it's cool — not everyone is so lucky. Is there anything else I can get you? No, thanks, we're all good! She floated away again, hoping we would enjoy our meals. We picked up our cutlery in unison and began to enjoy. The obligatory knifing of the runny egg yolk was imbued with a new, uncomfortable symbolism for me: instead of getting the aesthetic Instagram moment craved by visual creatures such as myself, I watched the carcass of the albumen gush sunshine blood on the grey, concrete-coloured plate and then duly become chalk in my mouth. No one else at the table saw what I saw and I supposed this to be the curse of the artist. Eggs were supposed to mean life. The arrival of casual brunch meant we didn't have to talk for a while, which was a blessing. And then it was over. With the last bite, my father reached into the depths of his jacket pocket and pulled out an official-looking envelope; the kind with the little plastic window showing the logo and the addressee. He passed it across the table with disinterested eye-contact. Above the type: PRIVATE AND CONFIDENTIAL, I could see the letter was open. I asked: Why is it open? but didn't wait for the answer. The opening sentence had me launched out of my chair in fight-or-flight mode. I was trembling quite violently and on the verge of tears. A newly arrived couple at the next table swivelled round beadily to look. My mother told me to sit down. In the commotion,

Paul took it upon himself to scrape the food bits and stack our plates neatly at the end of the table: I used to work in hospitality, he said. A different waiter, not Gothy this time, came to collect our plates. My father: Could we get the bill, please? No one said anything else. With nothing else to do, I resumed my seat, making entirely neutral eye-contact with Gothy across the beer garden as she deposited a tray of mimosas for a group of bougie uni girls. Somehow the restaurant had filled up around us, and I was overwhelmed by the sound of lubricated mouths eating and talking and the scribble of knives and forks on ceramic plates. Paul: It was absolutely lovely to meet you both. My father: It was good to meet you. My mother: It was interesting to meet you finally! When the bill arrived, the three of them performed the obligatory haggle, but I had neither the energy nor the financial capacity to meaningfully engage. I hadn't worked in weeks and the money I had accrued was granular in this economy. In the end, I think they agreed to split it. There were lots of smiles when the debit cards emerged and I felt small. All finished, we made our way outside the bar-restaurant and stood by the chalk patch and,

Cleaner

after agreeing that 'we must all do this again soon' in a chorus, my parents left. Paul and I watched them morph into two figurines in the distance, little dolls that didn't interact with each other. To the right of us, a solitary news cameraman packed away his equipment. I stared at the ground again. By now the busy shoppers and day-drinkers had kicked the bloody, chalky evidence away to almost nothing, and all police paraphernalia had been removed so as not to interfere with Saturday business. It was over. Paul turned to me: I said I'd go meet some friends, so I'll see you back at the flat... what was in the envelope? As pathetic as it was, I felt inundated with warmth at the basic human interest in my life: I've been invited for my first smear test. He did not seem perturbed and wished me congratulations before falling away into the slipstream of the crowd. I walked back through the city alone, bathed in a happy, unhappy sunlight. The train home was unremarkable, except for the fact I was tearful. It was only when I reached the front door to the building that I realised I didn't have a key. Luckily, the owner of the flat above took pity on me when I buzzed his doorbell. He escorted me up the stairs and along the corridor and was about to put the spare key Paul had given to him into the keyhole when he turned to me and said: Love, it's already open. It was true; the door was ajar. We contemplated it in silence. Do you want me to call the police? No, it'll be all right. I think we should call the police. No — I pushed the door open and strolled in while he stood stuttering in concern behind me. After surveying each room and confirming my suspicions that nothing had been stolen, I informed the neighbour everything was fine. He looked upon me with fear but ultimately nodded respectfully and left me alone. I took myself to Isabella and Paul's bed and masturbated myself into oblivion, dreaming she could hear me even though she was no longer here. How long had she been in the flat? What had she done? Why did she leave again? I must have slept because I woke into a purple night by the haze of the streetlamp filtering through the curtains. Paul was drunkenly clanging kitchen utensils and cupboard doors. He crept in, removed all of his clothes and for an endless moment stood over the bed watching me before cocooning his cool, heavy body over my blazing one. I dreamt of both Isabella and Paul that night:

they were playing themselves in the dream production, but their genitals were swapped for some reason. I didn't mind it. The next morning, I got up at dawn with the intention of painting the image of them. I made posh coffee in a cafetiere and brought it and an oversized mug to the studio, poured it luxuriously from a height, romanticising my life. Compared with my uni days, the conditions of my workplace were more than ideal. However, I did not paint. Sunday passed in a waste of sweat and boredom. On Monday at 7am, Paul informed me while lacing up his shoes that he was nipping to Bruges for 'a few'. A few what? I asked, but he didn't manage to say. I didn't like to push it when he already had his jacket on and was wheeling his mini-suitcase out of the door. He didn't look at me. Womanly intuition told me this could have been our first fight but I decided to be the cool-girl seeing as he had endured brunch with my parents. Also, he turned back to shrug and huff a little sigh that seemed to say: I don't really want to go. He looked deeply into my eyes and I dared to imagine the sheen of anguish at having to be called away from the place and person he wanted to be with the most. Then he spoke: Will you try and get the sun-dried tomato out of my good chinos? Yes, of course, I whispered demurely. His goodbye kiss left a pearl of organic blackberry jam on my lip and I thought about how that would make a great song lyric for my imaginary band. After Paul left, I sequestered myself within the sofa and watched the news, pointing the remote at the TV in slow motion, imagining I was in a DFS advert or similar, being a sexy wife. The trick is to tuck the feet into the sofa cushion to create optimum waist to hip ratio. I laughed self-consciously, even though I knew there was no one watching me. The news reporter droned: KNIFE ATTACK. Eight men had been arrested for the senseless murder of an individual outside a casual bar and restaurant in the city. (Goosebumps — I grabbed a nearby decorative scatter cushion to hug, somehow sensing what was about to happen next.) As they panned over re-used footage of the crime scene, I was stupefied to see myself on screen, standing casually beside Paul and my parents. It was only for a split second — it must have been just after we'd paid for brunch. I seemed appropriately morose (it was a good job I'd been crying) and I looked good in Isabella's dress standing next to a man like Paul. I looked unlike myself. I was about to ring my mother to tell her we were on the telly when the footage irritatingly cut to an image of the victim. The shock was instantaneous: I threw the cushion at the wall and leapt into the air. The Erotica Man! I'd know that moonscape face anywhere. It was The Erotica Man that was murdered! My first thought was that I'd trodden carelessly through (and complained about) his blood on my (Isabella's) shoes. The guilt was piercing. I searched the news story on my phone and found the tributes on his Facebook page. My second thought was that he did not look like his Facebook profile any more and, frankly, it was ridiculous his family and friends memorialised him on the world's stage with a photo clearly taken fifteen to twenty years previously. I turned back to the screen. The newsreader spoke about how he left behind a baby girl, and my initial shock suddenly bolted into panic. The Erotica Man: I still had his phone. I ran through the flat and into the bedroom, scouring all the surfaces. Where was it? I ransacked all the clothes in the wardrobe, the secret pocket in my Mr Darcy outfit, but no luck. It wasn't under the bed, or accidentally kicked under the bookshelf.

In the end I found it trapped behind the bedside cabinet and the wall. It was dead, of course, but that didn't deter me. I plugged it in and waited, stared at the nightmare mirror of myself on the black screen. Nothing was happening, so I began folding the clothes I'd thrown about the room neatly and returning them to the wardrobe. When the phone lit up and the buzzing vibrations started, I forced myself into the kitchen and made myself a frothy coffee so I'd have something to drink while I investigated the dead man's phone. Making myself walk patiently back to the bedroom took self-control I didn't know I possessed. I unlocked the phone (1234) but was careful to only view messages in the preview dropdown rather than opening them — I didn't want his family to think they were opened by his murdered ghost. The messages were mainly from 'Laura Fucking Bitchface': *the baby is at your mum's... why aren't you replying??... Hello???... will you stop at the... HELLOO DICKHEAD???* The messages were not as juicy as I'd hoped, and my coffee was bitter. I'd been hoping for clues as to their last conversation, the emotional skinning of exes clawing back scraps of dignity, messages from

Cleaner

Laura trying to contact her ex from beyond the grave. Instead the messages seemed no different from when I had read them before: disgruntled ex begging for adequate co-parenting. Perhaps The Erotica Man had bought himself a new phone in the days before his murder. But then again, I was only reading the message previews. There could be something. The upheaval of the morning now left me with the problem of what to do with the phone. Should I take it into the police station? Should I try to track down Laura Fucking Bitchface to return it? I thought about ringing Laura Fucking Bitchface but then I didn't want to alarm her when she'd see the caller ID as her murdered ex. Then I thought about ringing from my phone but realised that if I did somehow arrange to meet her, put the phone in her hand for her to peruse at her leisure and say 'this belonged to your ex', she would not only realise he'd titled her as 'Laura Fucking Bitchface' in his contacts but discover that he wrote shit erotica when I explained how in God's name I'd acquired his phone. The shit erotica! His magnum opus! I opened up the notes app with his story (complete with my editorial feedback) and emailed it to myself to ensure it wouldn't be lost to time. Preservation! Was I an archivist? An all-encompassing feeling I could not name permeated my consciousness, like my spiritual borders had been dipped in hot wax. This was probably the last thing he ever wrote or ever cared about writing. This was his baby. I had his baby, shit as it was, in my inbox. It was all a bit too much to contemplate. I decided to wait it out and left the phone in the bedroom to deal with later. The right answer would come to me. Today would be the day I actually did some painting, I decided. My area of interest would transpose into postmodernism with a preoccupation with technology, genitalia and selfhood. In the studio, I gave my usual greeting to Isabella's nude drawing of me before picking up a pencil to sketch some initial ideas. Half an hour later, there were a few muted etchings in silvery pencil but nothing had taken shape. No matter, I went to the kitchen and fixed myself a sourdough, beefsteak tomato, rocket, and balsamic glaze sandwich, ate it standing up over the kitchen island (because I was busy), and tried again. Minimal joy. I painted a cotton-candy-pink base on canvas, but the subject was yet to emerge. Craving stimulation, I texted a picture of the nude drawing of me to Paul. He replied almost instantly: *who's that?* (I was offended): *It's me. Oh. What do you think? You drew that? No. Oh? Isabella drew it. Oh.* He didn't respond much after that, even after I sent him a real-life photographic image of my tits: *nice.* Deflated, I re-sequestered myself on the sofa under the microfibre blanket and scrolled through endless tidying and sorting videos of *Blue Peter* mums on social media, re-organising their children's themed nurseries or decanting pasta and legumes into glass cylinders with pine lids. The internet is a wonderful place. I salivated over people changing their bedsheets, re-organising cumbersome electronic cords, dusting their minimalist apartments, steam-cleaning rugs and carpets. It was like drugs; the cleaning high was instantaneous, like real drugs, even if it wasn't as good as cleaning in person. I don't know how long I was in the rabbit hole. Without Paul, a body beside me, I was off-kilter and slightly paranoid. More than once I felt his phantom boner poking into my backside in the night. I slept, I woke, I watched. The sofa was a tumour attached to my side. (Or was I the tumour?) Either way, when the police came to the door, I wasn't sure how long it'd been: What seems to be the problem, officers? The rest was a blur. Once I told them where The Erotica Man's iPhone was (and they placed it carefully in a little plastic baggy like the movies), they invited me to the station and confiscated my phone. How could I refuse? I asked if I had time to shower before we went, as I'd been on the sofa for a while, but they said no, so I doused myself in clouds of Paul's deodorant. The taller police officer coughed rudely as we stood there in the bathroom: Ready? I'd recently watched a random throwback video of Paris Hilton and Kim Kardashian exiting a building and entering a car or vice versa and I hoped to channel this energy as I navigated the chasm between the front door of the apartment and the police car. My pointed walk over the symmetrical paving stones felt somehow symbolic and sensual. Equally, being driven through the city to the police station was an unexpectedly glamorous and luxurious experience behind tinted windows. The city seemed edgy and cosmopolitan behind the glass: the litter on grass corners had been tossed artfully, and hot daytime coffee-shop mums were vaping wintry plumes into the air. I asked the driver: Can we have the radio

Cleaner

on? No. Suddenly I was in the back seat of my parents' Skoda in the French countryside, trying not to be irritating. (Shit.) I wished I could've rolled down the window. I wasn't exactly sure where the nearest police station was but I knew it couldn't be too far. Naturally, when we arrived, the car door was opened for me, but there were no news people, like I'd hoped. It probably hadn't reached the papers yet. Equally, the opportunity for loitering in the street to stoke a media fire was limited — we'd parked as close to the entrance as possible, so I didn't get my dramatic entrance. The automatic doors whirred open and I was taken straight into a holding cell and offered water. Can I have squash? No. The door was closed and locked and I was very much stuck in the little cubicle. To pass the time, I started to sing hymns from my school days — Bread of life, Truth Eternal, Christ, Be Our Light, Here I am, Lord — before I was asked very nicely to be quiet by someone in a neighbouring cell who sounded like they were having a much worse day than I was. The place didn't seem that busy, however — business was slow on a weekday morning. After about an hour, I was called to the charge desk to give my details to a lovely young woman with unnecessary hair extensions. The arresting officer gave all sorts of official details which she clickity-clacked onto the computer keyboard. Onto biometrics next (the bit I was most looking forward to), where I was ushered into a little room to have my photograph taken by one of those strange black orb cameras latched to the wall. I tried doing my best defiant face, pretending I wasn't going down without a fight like Jane Fonda or something, but the officer had to tell me I was only allowed to do my normal face. My fingerprints were then taken on the machine and my DNA taken with a little mouth swab. It was proper cell time now: my home for the next 24 hours in police custody. Gearing myself up for a character-building, soul-rinsing ordeal, I kept my eyes closed as I entered the room picturing something out of Camus's *The Outsider*, but it was clean and fine. The room was tiled like a swimming-pool changing room, with a tiny bench bed and two flat blue cushions, like the gym mats from primary school. Somehow exactly what I expected but disappointing. Even the toilet was devoid of personality — it looked like the toilet from my parents' house.

Cleaner

The officer swung the thick metal door closed with a whine and a clunk and that was the only bit that resembled something from the telly. Instead of lying back and staring at the ceiling, I decided to get on with doing some press-ups and crunches but had limited success. There wasn't a bar for me to do pull-ups on, which I was secretly relieved about. I doodled a picture of a cat, had a wee, then took a nap. I was woken by the officer telling me I could use the consultation room to speak with a solicitor via phone call but I refused. Too embarrassing — I curled up on the bench again. The nap was surprisingly good in the cell. I woke up and felt like I was on holiday. Chicken Tikka Masala for dinner; clearly microwaved but not without flavour. Just as I was getting excited about spending a night in the clink, I was escorted to Interview Suite 3: a windowless room with carpet-like soundproofing on the walls in blue. The police force loves blue. Sitting down at the table, I was a bit saddened to see a television screen for filming where there should've just been a cream voice recorder with big buttons. The officer spoke: We'll start shortly. I asked if I could smoke a fag but this was denied, so I sat and waited patiently.

An attractive middle-aged detective came in wearing pinstripe trousers and a cosy smile. She started the recording and gave her police spiel before looking at me expectantly: So tell me, is this you? She held up an iPad with a screengrab of the newsclip with Paul and me stood outside the bar with the stray police tape fluttering in the breeze. *Yes, that's me!* She latched onto my enthusiasm immediately: Oh, yeah? One of our officers here just recognised you from the clip... Why were you there? Delighted, I started from the beginning, giving a brief overview of my life thus far; leaving education, finding Isabella in the bathroom of the art gallery (minus the cocaine) to eating casual brunch at the bar-restaurant with Paul and my parents. She was really happy things were going well for me — Paul's flat is lovely, she said, very modern, that's what my colleague who came to get you said. And how did you know Chris Gregory? That one threw me: Who? Chris, the man who owned the phone you had in your bedroom. Oh, is that his name? (To be fair, I had genuinely forgotten, as it's so generic.) I chuckled a little: What a boring name! The policewoman was suddenly a lot less friendly, her skinny noughties eyebrows

Cleaner

flattening over her eyes. Her voice curdled: Chris Gregory was murdered in a senseless attack, mobile phone notably absent from the corpse, and then this morning, his grieving ex-girlfriend and mother of his child receives an unexpected findmyiphone notification that Chris's phone has been unlocked in a luxury high-rise flat in the inner city. Equally, when we searched your personal mobile, we found repeated Facebook searches for the victim. Not to mention, of course, the plethora of artwork-dated days before the attack depicting violent murder, on display in your home studio with all the creepy handprints over the walls. Care to explain? I hesitated for what felt like an aeon, processing. The other officer looked me up and down silently and I was reminded of the time I hid my packed lunch in primary school because I wanted to try school dinners, so I invented a bullying conspiracy against myself, playing the thief of my own packed lunch. When the lie unravelled, I'd never felt shame like it. The teacher called my parents and me into a formal meeting to express their concern about my social skills. This wasn't as bad as that, at least. The detective took a heavy breath in: Failure to disclose evidence is a criminal offence. I recollected the screen watching me to my right and shuffled guiltily: I don't think you're going to believe me. She waited, sighed heavily. I apologised. Slowly, I told her all about my brother and the woman from Des Moines, who'd commissioned the cursed painting at the *Pride and Prejudice*-themed gender-reveal party by Isabella, where she and I miraculously re-united (minus the cocaine) before running away to the bar, where we met The Erotica Man (Chris), who gave me his phone and asked me for feedback on his erotica while we were drunk — the detective's face remained unmoved — I explained that, after the bar closed, Isabella and I got into a taxi and left him on the street and I didn't realise I had his phone until the next morning, but then I forgot about it until I saw his face on the news yesterday. The fact I'd happened to go for brunch at the scene of the crime was just one of those bizarre coincidences. I unlocked his phone because I was curious. I was curious. Incidentally, I also had a degree and masters in Fine Art and recently had to drop out of a PhD for financial reasons; I painted those bloody murder scenes the other week because I was on my period and feeling acute rage for the plight of women — it was meant to be symbolic. You can check the period tracking app on my phone. Silence. I breathed again. Despite the officer's upsetting coldness, it was gratifying to get everything off my chest while she made careful notes: What was the name of the bar? I told her. What time did you arrive, roughly? I told her. We'll probably need to speak to your friend, what's her full name? I don't know. Where does she live? I don't know... I don't really see her much any more. My cheeks bloomed with a warmth that I hoped the recording didn't pick up. The officers looked at each other like they knew something I didn't. When they asked how they might reach her, I gave them her phone number, as that was all I could honestly do. After a final pause the officer grimaced: Well, we'll chase your bar story up, hopefully CCTV will corroborate your account if we can't reach your friend. Thanks. I was taken back to the holding cell, where my cosy nap-cove had transformed into a hard, tiled freezer box. The blueness of the walls seemed to metastasise into the air, clinging to my body and I lay on the bench without sleeping — with every passing hour, I regretted my multiple naps and wept into the night alone. The only small comfort in that cold purgatory was the hour when moonlight shone, iridescent, onto the stainless-steel toilet, a pseudo night-light. How I slept, I don't know. In the morning the swinging scream of the metal door summoned me to the charging desk again. I was too wiped out to pay proper attention to what they were saying but I eventually got the gist that they were letting me go. Thanks for having me, I said. The officer gestured to the door and that was that — I was kicked out without a ride home. Being politely kicked out seemed more tragic than being escorted out. Tendrils of sunlight warmed my cheeks as I leaned against the metal barrier on the wheelchair ramp. Another day. Being taken in by the police, although initially promising, wasn't the cultural highlight of my year, as I'd hoped. The score of my life was coloured slightly grey as I marched to the bus stop — like a film before the diegetic sound is put in by the foley artists. Vacant. The bus was late and a group of teenage girls in uniforms beside me whispered loudly about my BO. Back at the flat, I fell onto the bed and slept through the rest of the day and night. I awoke gummy-eyed and heavy with woe. Had another little cry. With the purity of morning, I realised I was back where I'd started and desperately needed to replicate my steps. This was the halfway point of my story. Like last time, I started with the washing-up, finding myself emotional over the creamy ceramic plates and determinedly squeaking them clean. Then I dried them and put them away, disinfected the kitchen surfaces, took all the food out of the fridge, and organised it into colours, watered the plants, rearranged the tins in the cupboard, polished the cutlery in hot water and vinegar, took out the bins, put a cotton pad of essential oil under the bin bag, started a load of laundry, got the tomato out of the chinos, painted over the creepy handprints on the studio wall in duck-egg blue, mopped, wiped, sprayed, decanted, fluffed, sucked, spritzed, scrubbed, chiselled, wrenched, swept, closed and locked the studio door with a vow. Then I sat very still and tried not to touch anything in a meditative state. I had a bath, removed every single socially unacceptable hair on my body, dead-heading myself. Then I started on the bathroom, wiped the surfaces, took the toilet seat off, cleaned the mirror, dismantled and soaked the shower head, put the toilet seat back, wiped, sprayed, decanted, fluffed, sucked, spritzed, scrubbed, chiselled, wrenched etc. Paul returned at some point during this ritual (Anything interesting happen while I was away?) but I refused to let him touch me as I was clean. He seemed affronted and turned away to make a protein smoothie — I was reminded of something somebody said once about 'rubber band theory' to keep them keen. I put a frozen pie in the oven for him and logged into his MacBook to apply for jobs. Paul hid in the bathroom for a while. At midnight, he told me he missed me and reached out a childish hand. I held him under the covers and cradled his head, my breath navigating its way through strands of his hair, blowing them about like anemone in underwater currents. We didn't have sex, which surprised me. In the morning, Paul mumbled into my left breast how he didn't want to go to work and how he wanted to stay under the covers with me all day but I was very responsible and kicked him out. As a reward, I slept in long past noon, until I was so sweaty that the bedsheets were wet, forcing me to repeat the ritual of cleansing my body and cleansing

Cleaner

what it had contaminated. Pretending the morning wasn't a modern 21st-century waste, I found a wide-brimmed hat, flowery sundress and roomy wicker bag to dress up for the farmers' market. My goal for the day was to meander with intent, flâneuse-style. In anticipation of the park being full of picnickers and students and lovers on this sunny day, I took a long-shortcut through a little copse adjacent to the path to meaningfully observe without being seen — and to feel tiny and cute against the backdrop of silver birches. But the park was empty. I emerged from the bushes disappointed. Walking along the smooth, trimmed path out in the open, I became acutely conscious of the curated wilderness instead; the council had recently been pumping money into 'green spaces' and the 'wild' meadow was starting to look particularly organised. The insects seemed to sense the artificiality of the scene despite being the target (and desperately sought-after) demographic. More than once I saw a young summer bee reject an overly prominent and unnaturally large sprig of wild heather lolling pointedly over the edge of the meadow. Poor heather. Planted on display and past her prime, she seemed the equivalent of a flower prostitute. She wasn't a classy, discreet flower off the beaten track; she was being pimped by the council for bees and dog-walkers and award-hungry park-itects that couldn't care less about her wellbeing. Everything was advertising nowadays. Reaching the end of the path, I was then confronted with the aesthetic whiplash of the plastic, primary-coloured children's playground. The 'wild' park was soulless and the playground was packed. Where was the balance? The harmony? It wasn't just the waste of space that bothered me. The playground was choking with mums in synthetic-coloured cardigans monitoring and micromanaging their children's play. The children couldn't move for mothers. Where was the risk? The problem solving? It was all too false and bright and safe. In my discomfort, I exited the park running and ventured over the main road without looking. A double-decker bus had to brake sharply and I had to give the irresponsible pedestrian wave, *Sorry!* Then I minced down the hill at an appropriate stroll to my destination. The farmers' market was smaller than I'd assumed it was whenever I'd walked past it before, but still, there was something greatly comforting about browsing in the fresh air like my foremothers did. I wanted to haggle over a good cut of meat and for someone to stamp my ration book. The fruit vendors were as bloated and pufferfish and middle-aged and goblinesque as I'd imagined them to be, calling *come buy, come buy*. I took great joy in pretending to ignore each stall owner in favour of picking up palm-sized fruit to weigh in my hand and bring to my nose to sniff delicately in assessment. I'd hold, I'd weigh, I'd sniff and smile, then move on, elusive, as if I could sense something about that conference pear that no one else could; some secret, hidden grain of fault preventing me from purchasing. Unfortunately, by my third lap of the market, the stall owners caught on and I was abused for being a serial sniffer and I could either buy that fucking nectarine or have it stuffed up my — in the end I bought everything I'd sniffed out of guilt and was forced to pay for an industrial crate to carry it all back in an Uber. Lugging it up the stairs to the flat was a nightmare of Duke of Edinburgh proportions. More than once I was forced to pause, heart pounding, at crisis point. It would have been nothing to let myself tip back through space, ever so slowly and then all at once, to crush my vertebrae into pulp against the stairs. The vision was unnervingly seductive: I had to drink a cup of hibiscus tea and meditate upon the motion of taking each sip to bring myself back to my senses. I wasn't really interested in breaking my neck so much as in the image of falling. Later, when Paul returned from work, he questioned the fruit conceptually: What is this? I told him: Fruit. Yes, I can see that, why is there *so much* fruit? (He delved a hand into the crate.) Fucking hell, how much did all this cost? Cornered, I told him it was for art and he knew better than to ask. He went to the 24-hour gym for leg day without his dinner and I ate barbecue tempeh alone. Sat in the studio looking at the guilt-fruit afterwards, I was forced to confront the fact that I was weak. Isabella wouldn't have been. She'd have stolen the fruit at the first hint of an imbroglio, or pelted it at the stall owners until they were painted in juice. Then, when her enemies were vanquished, she would have turned on me, pelting me with pomegranates, blood oranges, peaches, nectarines, cherries, blueberries, mangoes, apples, all while glaring with the black seeds of her pupils contracted in disdain. Then (hopefully) she would have licked

Cleaner

all the sticky sweet detritus off my body head to toe and I would be purged of it all. Clean. Morning came in a rush of sunlight tide. I had been so locked within my imagination I had not seen the current of night ebb and eddy into day again. A documentary I'd seen once years ago resurfaced in my mind, about how the rotation of the Earth was slowing bit by bit. I'd imagined how one day billions and billions of years from now a single day on Earth would be 48 hours long and wondered whether any humans would survive a reality disparate from our evolutionary bio-clock. In many ways I felt like I was still stuck in the previous day; I'd sweated into the bedsheets, I'd washed the sweat off my body, I'd looked at the 24-hour clock already pushed past noon, and despised my modernity. I'd pondered over the wicker bag — couldn't face the market again. Instead I went to the park to examine and critique the playground more closely. Flâneuse-cum-sociologist. My thesis was correct: the playground might as well have been entombed in bubble wrap. Everything was plastic and tarmac and wood chippings and hand railings, and this is the way you climb through and not upside down and not too high please! Parents (mums) were poised like goalkeepers under the single-storey treehouse: watch your step, watch your step, that's it, watch your step, that's it! Watching these children was fascinating and akin to omniscience. In their little chubby heads I could see the mould of excessive caution blossoming on the inside of their tiny skulls. Hold on tight, hold on tight, HOLD ON! Later, when they start school or university, these mums will wonder why their children aren't self-sufficient and don't know how to function without approval. They won't know how to fail. Dizzy with fury, I collapsed upon the nearest bench and appeased the Duolingo owl to distract myself. When I made a mistake, the brightly coloured, graphic owl told me to be careful and watch out for this common grammatical misconception and was I in a fucking digital playground? I put my phone away and tried not to think. Fixed my gaze on a random child on the climbing frame and willed it to ignore its mother and keep climbing higher. I didn't realise one of the other goalkeeper mothers had sat next to me with her spawn, a sad little thing with an anxious crease forming between its eyebrows. The mum caught me looking and I realised my error too late. She did the mum-friend introductory smile, patted her child on the head: Isla's just turned three. Which one's yours? She glanced small-talkily towards the climbing frame. With hindsight I suppose I'd unconsciously dressed like the rest of them in a synthetic cardigan — the empty wicker basket at my feet looked sturdy and had lots of compartments for wipes and nappies and fruit snacks and dummies. I cringed: Oh, I'm not a parent... (the mum's gaze pickled in fear and disgust)... anymore. I'm not a parent anymore. I just come here sometimes... to remember... (the mum's gaze wilted in pity and comprehension). In character, I turned away and stared at the trees. Grieving people seek nature because it's a reminder that life will go on, even though nowadays climate change has ruined that. On cue, a duo of starlings danced and parted over the treeline metaphorically. Very lucky. Naturally, the The Goalkeeper Mum was struck with my grief: I'm so sorry for your loss... I can't even imagine... you're so brave. I smiled bravely at her. What was your little one's name, if you don't mind me asking, so I can say a prayer? Her name was... Isabella. Isabella — that's a beautiful name. Thank you. I'm sure she's waiting for you wherever she is. Thank you, I like to think so. We looked at each other with extraordinary intimacy. I was just managing to squeeze out a tear when I clocked Paul jogging round the corner in his long-distance running gear — he had the marathon coming up. We locked eyes against my best intentions and he started ambling over with a disarmingly feminine canter, wrists flopping all over the place. I was glued to the bench and couldn't move. Paul: You okay? What are you doing here? I stuttered spasmodically, cornered, until The Goalkeeper Mum answered for me: She came here to remember. (She turned to me.) Is this your…? I nodded, half-smiled. Goalkeeper Mum stood up purposefully to look at Paul: I'm so sorry for your loss, both of you. Paul: Our loss? Goalkeeper, knowingly: Your Isabella. Paul (to me): Isabella isn't gone forever? Goalkeeper: Of course she isn't, that's such a nice way to think about it (brief sympathetic pause). Well, I must be off, we've got music and sensory play booked in half an hour. She fastened her child into her buggy and wheeled off into the distance along with all the other mums presumably booked into the same session. The line of prams chugged away into the future and the playground became a ghost scaffold. On cue, a bird shat a tremendous load right onto the concrete in front of me, getting all over my mum-trainers. Presumably a moral nudge. I got to my feet with a sigh and told Paul I was sorry about the fruit. He told me it was okay without looking at me. (Forgiveness?) Compelled on the slow walk back, I confessed my desperate lie to The Goalkeeper Mum in a mad rush of embarrassment and he laughed so hard he had to stop, bend over, and wheeze. You're something else, I swear, he said, looking at me again. He held my hand and swung it back and forth the rest of the way home in pendulous reassurance. Back at the flat, Paul went for his post-run shower and I sat at the breakfast bar dreaming for a moment, until I felt my mum-top being lifted off from behind. I was effectively and expertly coaxed into the steaming bathroom with warm, breathy kisses on the back of my neck. How dirty! How clean! When he was rinsing the shampoo out of his hair afterwards, he told me his parents were visiting and that we probably couldn't get out of it but don't worry, they're not that bad. I nodded and understood, shivering in the corner waiting my turn to rinse. I'd been expecting something like this to crop up and, in truth, I was rather looking forward to it. People are often distilled into their most natural state of being in the company of their parents and I was eager to experience a purer Paul. I asked him: When are they coming? Next week, for my birthday — I was thinking we could host dinner at the flat and maybe you could cook something. You like cooking, right? Sure. I cosied up in a fluffy dressing gown with Paul's laptop to start planning my menu. Naturally, the dinner party needed something fresh and simple and elegant; if I overcomplicated it, I was sure to fail and ruin the evening and I was not going to be a failure host for a second time. Especially not in front of any parents. On the World Wide Web, I favourited and pinned some promising recipes that purported flavour via simplicity. A good start. I had plenty of time. When I checked my email I was also rewarded with a request for a Zoom interview for a childcare company: a daycare during the summer holidays for working parents, affectionately titled 'The FunFactory'. I didn't hate the idea of telling people I worked in childcare, especially seeing as it was a seasonal job. I could add the phrase 'for the

Cleaner

summer' onto the end of the sentence and pretend I was still a student with a degree to go back to in the autumn: I'm working in childcare *for the summer*. I went to sleep that night tied up in Paul's arms like I belonged there. I rose early to make him protein porridge with blueberries and maple syrup and pack him homemade minestrone in a flask for his day at the big office. After a quick kitchen reset wiping down the surfaces and mopping the floor, I dialled into my Zoom interview. Outfit-wise, it seemed a good idea to aim somewhere between 'casual CBeebies presenter' and 'generic office attire'. Bright and safe and maternal. I'd also spent the morning rehearsing the gentle yet firm tone of voice required for business with children, which I was entirely confident the interviewer would pick up on. I needn't have bothered. When I joined the call, the interviewer only had about ten minutes to talk before she had to get back to the rotten children. The only thing she was interested in was what I would do if I had a safeguarding concern (report to the designated safeguarding lead, obviously) and was I available to start straight away? I was. Great; if you send off for your DBS and sign the digital contract, you'll be able to start next week. I've emailed everything to you already. Sorry, gotta go, the clown's just arrived for the circus-skills workshop. Thanks! She ended the call. I filled in all the forms as necessary and then shut down the laptop to stare at the abysmal void of my own reflection for a while, sitting with the knowledge that I had a week of life and time to kill before I could say I had a job for the summer. What to do. Paint? No. Draw? No. Clean? No; there was no more mess to mess with, I'd drained the flat dry. I fantasised briefly about buying a large stack of ceramic plates and smashing them therapeutically and symbolically on the kitchen floor, barefoot and frenetic, before sweeping up the fragments to glue haphazardly onto canvas. That would have been more original. Instead I went to the local shopping centre to purchase three volumes of adult colouring books and a bumper pack of grown-up felt-tip pens. New paper and pens evoked the feeling of a fresh September start. I whisked home the bounty and sat cross-legged on the rug in front of the coffee table (I had a fantasy of finally achieving the full lotus) to mindfully colour. And mindfully colour I did — aside from the general maintenance of the domestic sphere and my emotional obligations to Paul, I did not stir from that rug. I coloured in with such animated mindfulness that by the weekend I had essentially given myself repetitive strain injury and Paul had to hide the felt-tips against my will. The scene was somewhat ugly; we ended up playing a bizarre game of tug-of-war in the living room until I relinquished the pens out of emotional obligation and an inability to grip effectively due to the repetitive strain injury. Paul wore a greasy smirk on his face for the rest of the evening and I sulked because he and I both knew he was only saving me from myself. All sexual activity (masturbatory or otherwise) had to be sans wrist-action during my recovery. Luckily, I recovered just in time for Paul's birthday and was allowed to wank him off in the morning before preparing my menu: gazpacho, oyster mushroom paella, flan. I asked to have the flat to myself so Paul obligingly went to play golf with his money/data/finance/computer men. Don't be too long! Assembling the rainbow-coloured mise en place across the granite countertop was nothing less than life-affirming. I was balls-deep in 'operation wife-material'. Not that I actually wanted to be

Paul's wife, but rather I wanted Paul's parents to want Paul to want me to be his wife. I wanted approval. Entering the cooking frenzy clenched me into a ball of anxiety which only one thing could release; with Promethean foresight, I'd known to prepare dishes that could be made well ahead of time so that I could enjoy cleaning up afterwards at leisure. During the cook however, I found myself mitigating discomfort by edging my hygienic tendencies. I started by flicking wildly with dripping utensils to see how many of the splash-tiles I could cover and ended with flinging all the discarded vegetable peels over my shoulder to see what patterns I could make on the floor. All this made for a very satisfying clean and tidy in the aftermath. Straightening up the flat for real-life guests also provoked real innovation beyond the basics. Deep-cleaning the sofa was particularly satisfying; by soaking a microfibre cloth in hot water and washing-up liquid and attaching it to the bottom of the spray mop, I was able to score cute pinstripes running vertically along the velvet sofa cushions. Above the shower, I hung a delicious bundle of eucalyptus for aromatherapeutic purposes. By 6pm the flat effused 'Airbnb in the city' and was crowned accordingly with a fresh Yankee Candle (desert blooms). In the perfect-wife hierarchy, I felt on a par with the Virgin Mary — I bet she kept a beautiful home. As a schoolchild, I would spend hours thinking about the way she'd lovingly crush spices in a pestle and mortar, or how she swept the floor before the angel Gabriel interrupted her morning, or the kinds of packed lunches she'd make for Jesus. Paul got back from golf late and got straight in the shower before I could give him his present. He was initially confused, standing naked in the doorway: Why is there a fucking tree in the shower? Because it's nice! He huffed limpidly and slouched away again. The unravelled anxiety ball following the flat-spruce was winding up again with momentum. I had to sit waiting on the floor so I wouldn't disrupt the sofa lines, and counted the dripping of the tap. The parents were due for charcuterie imminently and I'd forgotten to practise any hostessing in the mirror. Too late now. Paul emerged with a wet Hugh Grant mop on his head just as the doorbell rang: Here we go. I thought it best to wait over the stove looking busy, then turn over my shoulder mid-stir, as if caught by surprise: Hi, nice to meet you! They weren't what I expected. They seemed nice. Neutral. As they mooched around the coffee table, I was reminded of cardboard cut-outs or photo stand-ins you get at the seaside. Parent bodies; insert face here. Paul hugged them with more enthusiasm than I expected and vice versa; in fact, they both held him in a kind of nativity pose, stood over him from behind as he sat on my sofa lines, their little boy all grown up. I approached them with the charcuterie board and, with my most winning smile, told them how pleased I was to meet them at last and that I definitely could see the family resemblance, nodding towards Paul. Then I learned Paul was adopted. I decided to give him his birthday present to change the subject. It's nothing much, I said. It really wasn't anything much because I'd paid for it with my own money. It was an impractically small mug with a cartoon stick man at his computer on it saying: *Don't talk to me, I'm coding!* Paul liked it so much he took it straight to his desk to keep his pens and pencils in. A mesmeric omniscience overcame my senses and I spoke about how I knew he would do that, how I had foreseen that he would use the mug as a kind of vase for his bouquet of writing implements. His parents glimmered in the candlelight: Paul said you were imaginative. Their sweet birthday man returned smiling and was handed his second present by his father. (This is from both of us, son.) It was a home foot spa because he was doing so much running now, he needed to look after his feet. Paul hugged them again, except this time he leaned over the pair of them seated on the sofa, subverting the nativity tableau, and I was moved. They had acted out before me, in essence and miniature, the last twenty-five years or thereabouts. Paul the boy, receiving unconditional parental love, and Paul the man, able to return it freely. What was this if not growth? They were still hugging long after the conclusion of my philosophical musing. I cleared my throat. It was my job to guide us all into the next phase of the evening, as the hostess, and I did: Shall I open the wine then? Resounding yes! Because Paul hadn't seen his parents in so long, the conversation over dinner was full and I took a supplementary witness role, which I was more than content with. The food slipped down their gullets without complaint and I received every generic compliment that indicated success. I must have the recipe for x… y must have taken hours… z is an absolute triumph — really delicious! After the flan was well received, I was finally able to sit properly at the dining-room table to enjoy the wine with gusto. Too much gusto. Worming myself into the conversation created a jump cut and suddenly I was talking emphatically without fully knowing what I was talking about. The candle had gone out and Paul was nowhere to be seen. The generic parents urged me to continue: Please, go on! Sorry, what was I talking about? You were talking about life modelling at the gallery where you met Isabella. I was talking about Isabella? Do you know Isabella? They smiled at my question, tipping their heads in unison. The father: Of course we know Isabella, she's a nightmare! The mother: Of course she's a nightmare, she's an *artist*. We laughed and laughed. Father: Everyone knows artists are huge egotists with low self-esteem, it's a deadly combination. Ha ha ha. Mother: 'Artist' sounds better than 'unemployed', though, ha ha ha. You're not an artist, are you? Well, I'm a cleaner but I'm moving into childcare for the summer. Oh… hm… And what do your parents think about that? The artlessness of their faces had transmogrified into something else without my realising. Their genericism hadn't changed but their look was suddenly shark-blank. I choked on the air. *What do your parents think?* My dry mouth parted with the answer: My parents think... they think that... I don't know whether I got the words into the air because they were laughing insincerely in the way only bespectacled, mawkish people can. They smiled and smiled these big strawberry grins that grew off their faces into big red crescent moons that parted into bloody vampiric emblems — and then I woke up, hanging off the side of the bed with a desert mouth and an aching head. The blackout blinds held a fire square of sunlight at bay, which made me nervous. I reached for my phone to check the time and my hand shook, indicating symptoms consistent with a diagnosis of trepidation and/or an apocalyptic hangover. My anxiety was appropriate. I was running late and my first day at the daycare started in less than 45 minutes. No sign of Paul. I pulled on the clothes that were lying on the floor and ran out of the flat without a second look. Got the bus to 'FunFactory BaseCamp' (the local primary school renting out the premises for the summer) and arrived with seconds to spare, stomach churning. I was greeted by a pruney, stuck-up woman on door duty (not the woman who interviewed me), who berated me for not turning up early to help set up, despite the fact I wasn't going to be paid until now. She set me up on the company app to log my hours and handed me a too-small branded neon T-shirt before kicking me into the main hall: First activity starts in ten minutes, by the way. I turned back to ask her a million questions about how to do this job but she was gone. I had to face the room headlong and was immediately overwhelmed; pint-sized children zigzagged amid Lego and colouring-in and Jenga and plastic dinosaurs; ebullient branded neon staff shouted instructions and organised colourful rucksacks and water bottles in rows by the wall; flecks of spit and snot and God only knows what else peppered the floor at my feet. My stomach jolted and the hangover permeating from my head to my stomach suddenly became a high priority. All this overstimulation occurred in a single split second, the last of personal freedom for the next eight hours. I was immediately latched onto by the leg: Toilet! Toilet! Toilet! I didn't know where

Cleaner

the toilets were, so I sought out the nearest branded neon person (who I later discovered was a sixth-former) and they pointed down the hallway: Are you taking a group to the toilet? Great. Hands up if you need the toilet? A forest of tiny arms lifted into the air to my dismay. I led them along the corridor in single file. If I wasn't so hungover, I'd have probably been overcome with nostalgia at the sight of the artwork displays and murals on the walls. Similarly, the toilets were so tiny and shrunken for tiny shrunken people that it was difficult to believe I was once so tiny and so shrunken. They filed in and out, chatting to each other and themselves the entire time, and I wondered at what age narrating yourself through your life becomes unfashionable. Unfortunately, there was no soap in the tiny shrunken sinks, so they couldn't wash their tiny shrunken hands properly and then the dryer wouldn't work, so they couldn't even dry their tiny shrunken hands properly. They clamoured wetly but I had nothing to give. Desperate and out of my depth, I told them to wipe their hands on their trousers and quick, let's go back and play! My hangover had become a ticking time bomb. I led the children into the main hall, just as they were being gathered into the middle to hear FunFactory rules and be auctioned off into red, blue, green, and purple groups. There wasn't time to ask a branded neon person where staff were supposed to go to the toilet. I ran back through the corridor and locked myself in a cubicle. Throwing up violently in a tiny toilet was a new low point. The sight of my giant hands gripping the miniature toilet seat created another causal link to my childhood, which I couldn't quite place. After several minutes of horrible retching, I was able to stand myself upright again and, reeling from the expulsion, the answer presented itself: looming over the cubicle walls, I was a perverted Alice in Wonderland. This made me laugh acidly, in spite of everything. Crouching to adjust my green, peaky face in the tiny shrunken mirror only took a few seconds. I steeled myself as best I could before heading back into the main hall where Pruney was waiting to chastise me, wrinkling her nose: Where have you been? Blue group are waiting to start making mini-gardens! Mini-gardens? She handed me a damp sheet of A4 with the activity specifications on it and launched me into the playground with a humongous

Cleaner

bag of soil. My sixth-former colleague arrived with a pile of small biodegradable trays and told the children to go off and find treasures while we lined them. Gormless and slightly in awe, I copied the sixth-former, shovelling soil with a blue plastic cup to create the bases of these so-called mini-gardens. When the children returned, babbling away about their treasures of rocks and pebbles and leaves and sticks and a stray button and a bead of glass and a dandelion wrenched from its roots, the sixth-former produced PVA and lolly sticks and had them fashioning picket fences on the borders of their gardens. After the tumult of the scavenge, they all sat rather nicely in the shade arranging their mini-gardens the way they wanted them. Occasionally, one would go foraging for the finishing touch (a rare feather discarded by an unwitting bird, an emaciated plastic bottle head) but mainly they stayed in the courtyard; glueing, organising, arranging. A kind of psychical paralysis clawed at my innards, witnessing the scene. My immediate instinct was to question the children on their curative choices and offer them guidance, as was my paid role and graduate expertise, but I maintained a cool distance. My incessant adult sensibilities would suffocate the learning. I knew myself, I knew I would monopolise. When I consulted the damp sheet of A4, there were no real pedagogical guidelines to follow, so I stayed on the outskirts of the artistic circle, sentinel, which felt lazy. A small acorn of a child nestled in the womb of the tree looked through me as if sensing my dilemma. As much as I wanted them to innovate independently, I didn't want to leave them without support. How would they know I was interested in their work if I didn't get involved? The little girl squirmed on her makeshift seat, evidently engorged with artistic fury; she needed something, some relic, some totem that was missing from her garden composition. I decided all I needed was a sincere invitation to join the world of childish discovery and smiled as best I could. She opened her mouth: Toilet! My hangover slouched and groaned inside me. Being out in the fresh air had been restorative — I wasn't sure I'd survive another journey to the tiny shrunken place. When I appealed to the gaze of the sixth-former, I found no comradeship. Resigned, I found the last of a packet of peppermint chewing gum in my pocket and prayed it would hold more vomiting at bay. Come on, then. We made the journey down the corridor with her little sprout of a hand nestled in mine. I zoned out to stave off nausea and only resurfaced when the child in question wailed from within the cubicle. She wanted her mummy. I didn't know what to tell her. Something about the tone of her voice made me bite back the tears a little as well, I thought maybe I had done the same thing in school once. Come on out now, she'll be back before you know it! I felt then that there are two types of people in life: those who cry in school for their parents or for themselves and those who do not. I wondered what it was that made me the former. Maybe I was born with it — maybe I was just hungover. The rest of the day transmuted into what felt like an aeon of snack-times and brain breaks and lunch-times and free-times and activity-

times and carpet-times; all of which essentially involved me careering blue group into whatever corner of the premises they were supposed to be occupying. They were docile enough; I got better at befriending them, but I was still clearly an amateur and the children sensed this. Their questions towards me were stilted and acerbic, like they were the ones coaching me on how to converse with unfamiliar people. Even on my twenty-minute lunch break with the sixth-former, my conversation was flaccid. Once we'd gone past how I was just doing this for the summer for a bit of extra cash, I had nothing else to offer for the remaining nineteen minutes. She had to carry both of us with an anecdote about getting pizza delivered to the sixth-form college campus and getting a disciplinary. Late afternoon unrolled itself languidly. One by one, parents arrived for pick-up, while us neon folk cleared and swept away the sandwich crumbs and bogies and lost toy parts. The last children were relegated to 'quiet corner' while we disinfected the dinner tables with watered-down surface cleaner and J-Cloths (unsatisfying). Then it was over. The last collection of the last child left the hall in an eldritch silence. Pruney appraised us conservatively: Good work today, guys! Remember to come in early to set up tomorrow for festival day! The sixth-former very kindly drove me to the bus stop because of course she had a car and could drive it and I didn't because… well. I got back to the flat around 7pm and lay on the sofa,

Cleaner

utterly depleted. Paul rounded the corner from the office and said hello and I freaked into the air like a spooked cat. Somehow in the sensory overload of my day I'd forgotten he existed, that this was, in fact, his flat and not mine. The shameful question mark hanging over the previous night seemed to bob over him in my imagination like he was a Sim from the Sims or something (in the Apartment Life expansion pack, naturally). He spoke in a voice that betrayed nothing, no meaning, no emotion. I couldn't understand him, it was a different language. After getting him to repeat himself, with no success, I tried to remain calm: I'm sorry, what did you say? I SAID ARE YOU OKAY? Oh. I told him I was fine. He was too exhausted from his day at work to probe any further — valid. We sat for several moments. Over the tumbleweed my stomach bubbled, unhappy. I asked him in my nicest voice if he would please make me some tea and toast, because I hadn't eaten all day and I couldn't move, and he did. Manna from heaven. After delivering half the loaf to me, shuttling back and forth from the toaster, Paul sat down again and put some generic contact sport on the television. He asked about my first day at daycare and I recounted the headlines. Do you think you're going to stick with it? I don't know. He turned back to the TV and I went back to my toast. It was one of those moments where we should have been holding hands but we weren't. Eventually, the butter lubricated my mouth enough to let me ask about the previous night with his parents and all that wine. What had happened and what I said. Paul seemed surprised I had little memory after the flan: I don't know… you got very quiet and then all of a sudden you excused yourself, told my parents it was lovely to meet them and took yourself off to bed. That was it. That was it? I waited for the surprise to give way to relief but it didn't happen. I questioned him again: I didn't embarrass myself? No… Why… Did you think you did? The glint of mischief in his eye did not cheer me. I covered my face to hide my incomprehensible emotions because they were somehow tearful ones. I held his hand: What did they think of me? I don't know… they said you were nice enough — they said you made the flat look beautiful. Oh. But if they didn't like you, they would have said. Oh, okay. My poker face has always been poor but, luckily, Paul didn't notice. That night

Cleaner

I dreamt I was stuck inside a mini-garden and couldn't get out. My miniature feet couldn't get purchase on the lollipop-stick fence when I tried to climb over the top and, when I dug through the soil with my miniature fingers, all I reached was the bottom of the biodegradable tray. My only hope was to be saved. Suddenly, in my dream, the sun was blocked by the giant, Godlike figure of a child come to arrange the garden with its tiny-enormous chubby fingers. I appealed to it for help, gesticulating wildly and jumping, but it did not see me. Only when I wailed and cried with anguish did it look in my direction blankly — with Isabella's face. I woke up in need of comfort. Paul patted me on the head with good intentions while I quivered with longing. Standing under the baking-hot shower spurred me into action and I was able to give the flat a quick refresh before heading into work early to help set up for festival day. The morning sun painted the concrete gold and it felt like it was going to be a good day. Pruney was somehow still unhappy with me, even though I was the first and only employee present at the stipulated time. Alone, I set up the collapsable canteen tables, the sensory tent, the toy station, the gym mats, the reading corner. All of this I did with vim and vigour to atone for yesterday's unprofessionalism. When the children started to arrive, enthused in their party clothes, tutus and special T-shirts and sunglasses and light-up trainers, I made a point of sitting at the table and colouring in within the lines without making any attempt to acknowledge or greet them. Curious, they gravitated towards my feigned indifference. Before the first activity, I made a point of learning all their names properly and by noon everyone wanted to hold my hand and sit on my lap. By early afternoon, I had six original crayon portraits of myself gifted to me, signed by the artists in spiky misshapen scrawl. Basking in childish love, the idea of parenthood lurking in the centre of the adult maze finally seemed worth finding. The bouncy castle arrived on the field and Pruney gathered the neon people to hear their pitches for what role they wanted for the festival, like it was 'The Apprentice'. I made a strong, confident pitch for face painting, citing my extensive postgraduate experience in the arts — and won. I thanked Pruney for the opportunity and told her I wouldn't let her down. It made sense to set up my station in the main hall, where the disco would be taking place (a central location with good footfall), so I picked a corner and laid out all the paints and sponges and brushes and water. An excitable queue formed immediately and the first lucky child sat down before me to describe their vision of themselves as a Pokemon. I can do that, close your eyes... After a quick google, I took the plunge with the first brushstroke and let my instinct do the rest. I didn't have a wide range of colours but acted on my own initiative and adapted the palette accordingly. Eyes closed and cherubic, the child twitched with anticipation: Am I done yet? Almost! I twirled the finishing touch and held up the mirror in front of him: Open! He opened his eyes and gazed at his reflection... impassively. He didn't like it. He stood up to go play musical bumps. What do you say? Thank you. No time to feel: the next child seated themselves down, begging for a monkey. No problem! After my cursory google, I sponged the base on their face madly. That tickles! Keep still! Canvas and the contours of a face were very different from each other. When the child told me she was about to scratch her nose because she had no choice, I blew cool breath over her on autopilot, knowing that someone did the same to me at a summer fete once. It was the same breath somehow. She giggled musically. When I held the mirror up for her, I felt confident, but her face fell too. What do you say? Thank you. She wandered off outside towards the bouncy castle, rubbing her eyes. No time: the next child wanted a sheep. Close your eyes, that tickles, disappointment, what do you say? Dinosaur. Close your eyes, that tickles, disappointment, what do you say? Fairy. Close your eyes, that tickles, disappointment, what do you say? Spiderman. Close your eyes, that tickles, disappointment, what do you say? Lion. Close your eyes, that tickles, disappointment, what do you say? What do you say? What do you say? What do you say to a disappointed child? At the end of the shift, once the bouncy castle had been fully deflated and loaded into the van, I informed Pruney I was quitting. It wasn't for me. Okay, you'll need to return your uniform by this time next week or it'll come out of your wages. Fine. I walked out into the piss-gold sunshine without turning back. Sixth-former didn't give me a lift this time, so I had to get the bus home. Town had become a bland, artificial city and not the vibrant metropolis I remembered as a child. Cutting through the shopping centre, I was approached in slow motion by two bug-eyed women who slowed me to a stop by a kind of mind control. They were dressed conservatively in pastels and florals. Only one of the pair spoke, while the other watched the other one speak, not in a way that indicated a power imbalance but, rather, that it was just the taller one that happened to be the mouthpiece of them: Excuse me, they said. (I assumed they were going to ask for directions.) Yes? Excuse me, can I ask, do you have faith? Either the question or the sincerity of their countenance drew an unwitting answer from me about my Catholic upbringing and how my parents' divorce from the Church during my early teens left me an insecure non-believer housed within a consciousness forged and formed from the rigidity of Church and sin. The women nodded in unison: Can I ask, what is your purpose? Again, I answered honestly, and with no instinct towards self-preservation, that maybe I had replaced Church with school and university because I needed something to worship. The women, nodding: Are you happy? Something like fear corroded the inside of my throat and chest: I don't know, I said, lying and telling the truth simultaneously. Gathering that they were Jehovah's or Mormons or something I waited for them to start their holy spiel and hand over a leaflet for me to politely decline, but there was nothing. Absolutely nothing. They stared at me with their bug eyes and I was completely convinced in an instant that they were planted there on purpose by something beyond human comprehension. The longer the pause drew on, the more unreal I felt. Tonelessly, I uttered that I was in a bit of a rush actually and that I would be going on my way now, thanks. Absolutely nothing in response. They stayed stock-still, smiling, in the same position, even after I walked away. I know because I turned around to check and was horrified at the image of them standing and waiting, with their backs turned. I hurried back to the flat as fast as I could and hid under the covers, convinced that, if I lifted the duvet an inch, I would see them standing there waiting by the wardrobe with nothing to say. Under the duvet I was safe. They found me in my nightmares instead; sitting on the sofa in a shrunken Victorian-pauper version of my parents' living room, waiting.

Cleaner

After three days hiding, Paul suspected indolence on my part, despite my efforts to explain to him that I was entrenched in the throes of fight or flight. He made me tell the story again, which didn't help, as I could hear how ridiculous I sounded, which only upset me further. Never mind! The tears were hot and shameful. I made lasagne from scratch in an attempt to placate Paul and placate my own sensibility. It worked to a degree. Paul condescended to have regular, run-of-the-mill sex with me that night — but we didn't speak. The next morning, we had basic sex again and it felt filthy but not in a fun way, more like we were pugnacious bacterial cells jostling in a petri dish. It was only afterwards that he said he was sorry for being brusque and I said sorry for being a wimp. I also confessed to quitting my job at the daycare because my manager was horrible (not a lie), and he said that was a shame because I was so keen to begin with. We spent the day in a kind of hologram; acting out homemakers and lovers and performing the housework together in perfect harmony. We had a small disagreement over what film to watch in the evening, which only seemed to make the routine more charming. At 4am, when I couldn't sleep, I refreshed my CV and sent it out into the world again, a girlish wish into the night. Then I took myself into the living room and dragged an armchair to the window to gaze up at the stars and feel things. It was too cloudy. When I awoke, I was swaddled in the bed again and Paul was not there. In the living room, the chair had moved back to its usual place all by itself. No jobs on the computer. With nothing to do and nowhere to go, I sat and did nothing. I did not exist. My spirit became clogged with the psychic equivalent of fast food and cheap beer and I wasted two days in a mire of self-loathing. With no distractions to speak of, the gravity of the failed face-painting fiasco, the truth of why I couldn't return to the FunFactory DayCare, sank me down even further. Not because it was so catastrophic my depression was justified, but rather each failure was so small and localised that the ensuing incapacitation felt even more pathetic: what hurts more, a grown-up stab wound or a thousand tiny paper cuts? What's supposed to hurt more? I took a bubbleless bath and couldn't move for sadness. I didn't realise how long I'd been there until Paul burst in and yelled in horror. He thought I was dead because I was so cold and still and my eyes were closed, because I'd fallen asleep. It was very romantic — I felt like Ophelia. Paul made me stand under the hot shower to get warm again and passive-aggressively thrust a cup of hot chocolate into my hands afterwards: Maybe you should go to the GP or something. No, I'm just being silly, honestly. Once Paul was asleep, I wrapped myself up warm in a big hoodie and went venturing out into the night, like I did before I moved back home. My emotions needed a reshuffle or a shock. On the streets, I instinctively pretended I was in a true-crime podcast, turning each midnight corner with reckless abandon, waking up my body with fear. I read something once (I listened to an influencer 'doctor' lecture on TikTok) about how your body doesn't know the difference between thoughts about things happening and things happening in reality, which is why anxious people will wear their bodies out and die earlier, even though they are worrying about that exact thing. In the spirit of this, I thought about screaming, even though no one was really attacking me. Then I thought about the neighbours and decided against it — it wasn't fair to disturb them when they were all tucked in, marinating for their 9-to-5s. In a kind of gentle teleportation, my feet navigated their way to the park of their own accord, to the bushes and trees at the bottom of the hill. Where I expected silence, I found noise. From a distance the plastic children's playground was teeming with life: a group of hoodied individuals were lolloping carelessly in shadowy blobs, smoking cigarettes that crackled orange, lighting up their strident laughter. I felt a short, sharp urge to run up the hill and join in, but then remembered I was too old now and that it wouldn't feel the same because I didn't have my parents on hand to lie to about where I was and what I was doing. I'll never get to be that kind of teenager, because that time has gone. Above the scene, the white fingernail moon smiled and kept her eyes closed. I watched the shadows lounge on the swings, go down the slide head first, acting out a different kind of youth from their daylight companions. Joyful rebellion. All at once, a baptismal rain coated the world in a providential rush. The hoodied blobs shook their arms in frustration and pushed and shoved each other towards shelter. I waited for the noise to completely die away before making my approach, trudging up the hill against the downpour. In the dark and the rain, the plastic falseness of the playground was diluted and I could actually assess the composition of it; how the trajectory of the playing child had been thought through, from the climbing frame into the slide into the roundabout into the swing. Looking at it now, the scaffolding for childish imagination wasn't so offensive. If only the patronising colours, the plastic, didn't exist. A morsel of an idea, mischievous, scampered its way to the forefront of my consciousness; if I couldn't change the plastic, at least I could disguise it. Only interesting people giggle in the park in the dark in the rain. I ran home in an ecstatic gallop. In my absence, Paul's flat had become cosy and appealing again, and not a wasteland to die in. I ran around in my trainers making muddy pathways across the lino and gave in to the urge to shake out my soaking hair all over the floor like a naughty dog. Then I mopped like the angel in the house. Domestic Jekyll and Hyde. I changed into dry pyjamas and made tea, curling up on the sofa to watch YouTube videos on how to crochet. Desperate for material, I cut a couple of old T-shirts to ribbons, which worked unexpectedly well. Immediately (in my mind), Paul stretched into the room, yawning with the dawn, and I realised I hadn't slept. All around me the T-shirt ropes were splayed out in nonchalant greeting. Paul did a double take: Are those mine? I made us beans on toast and allowed myself a two-hour power nap before heading out to Hobbycraft for actual supplies. When I returned, I got straight into bed, sniffling with a cold after my chilly escapade the day before. The rest of the week was spent either in bed recuperating or locked in the studio weaving yarn, cutting tarpaulin, tying knots into the rigging of my design. I became a spider in a woollen web. Paul wasn't allowed to enter my domain but was permitted to deliver cups of tea and biscuits to the threshold and signal their arrival with a knock. The only time I left the flat was to visit the park with an industrial measuring tape to calculate the dimensions of my design. Unfortunately, I arrived during the afternoon when the goalkeeper mums and their bubble-wrap babies were there, so I had to measure around them, but I don't think I was too much in the way. When I glanced over to The Goalkeeper Mum I had spoken to the other

Cleaner

week, the one who was kind, I smiled normally, like a normal person. Instead of smiling back properly, she looked me up and down in a syrupy manoeuvre and whispered into the ears of the other mums. They all nodded in polite recognition and smiled at me in the same way. I was confused, rejected, until it dawned sickly and stained upon me — I wasn't part of their club. Perhaps they thought I was completing a remembrance project for my (fake) deceased child that they were too squirmy and British to ask questions about. By their stares I could tell they were interested, but they did not deign to speak this interest. A rage on behalf of the grieving consumed me. If I had really been a bereaved parent, and if baby Isabella had really existed, I would have been irreconcilably scarred by this snub. It didn't matter that I wasn't telling the truth. How dare they stigmatise and exclude a grieving mother! How dare they think my grief would contaminate their cookie-cutter lives! The fury had me winding and knotting my crochet project faster than I'd ever worked before. It didn't matter what the art meant as long as it got done; I visualised the time spent working and saw a long wispy yarn of time well spent stretching off into a desert plain. Yarn infiltrated my dreams. All the fine delicate work strained my eyes more than I could cope with and I had to commandeer Paul's reading glasses for the final stretch. But I wanted to get it done and I did. The night I was to execute my secret plan arrived with a gift: Paul had caught my cold and was coughing like an old witch. I made us immunity-boosting soup for dinner and we watched a cooking show while we ate it, because it's not enough to cook and eat your own dinner, you have to watch other people cook dinner and do it better than you. When Paul asked if I was coming to bed, I said I was going to sleep on the sofa, because I was worried his coughing would keep me awake (not a lie). He said all right then and slumped away, all sniffles and droop. I had already packed everything ready in suitcases to transport to the park so it was just a matter of waiting for Paul to fall asleep — a moment which I wildly misjudged. When I was wheeling the suitcases quietly along the corridor from the studio, a nasal, whipcrack voice snapped me round. The landing light flicked on, police-bright, to reveal Paul in the doorway. I dropped the suitcases in a thump. Are you leaving

Cleaner

me? He looked incredulous rather than distraught. I told him that I was just going out for a walk. With two suitcases? I sighed, and deliberated over which was the easier option: to confess the truth or to go along with the break-up narrative. In the end, Paul decided for me. He grabbed the suitcases and unzipped them with histrionic flourish. He stared at the contents with no discernible reaction to what he was seeing. I said something bold along the lines of 'if he loved me, he wouldn't question me', but he asked me lots of questions anyway about what the fuck I was up to and what was all this crochet for. Defeated, we returned to the breakfast bar and I explained my plan to make the playground a more magical and less sterile place. How I wanted the children to play amongst something beautiful and special. How I wanted to give them something anonymously with no conditions, like I was some kind of garden fairy, elves-and-the-shoemaker-style. Paul fixated on the wrong bit: But don't the shoemaker and his wife give the elves clothes to say thank you? Yes, but that's not the point! The longer I talked the less conviction I had in my vision. Paul seemed to sense this and asked too many practical, logical questions: What would happen if a child got tangled up in the yarn when they were climbing and hurt themselves? What if one of those kids that smoke in the park sets light to it? What would happen when the yarn got wet and started to rot? How would I feel if the kids didn't like it and pulled it all down? I hung my head, humiliated. Paul shushed me gently, holding my hand: I think you need to find a new job, a proper job and actually stick to it. Fixing other people's stuff isn't going to make you happy. When I was done crying, he led us to the bedroom and coughed all the way through our lovemaking. The blowjob was particularly difficult but I persevered. In the morning, I took a pair of scissors to my misguided yarn creation and cut it to pieces so I wouldn't be tempted by any more professional time-wasting. Then I logged into the computer and looked at my email to see if any of the jobs I applied for were successful — nothing — and sent out another batch, trying to manifest success but only able to think about the blackness of space and the orbital trajectory of the Sun around the Milky Way and how she was dragging us all nowhere, forever. Determined to stay calm, I washed the duvet covers, hand-scrubbed an old period stain on the mattress protector, bought dinkelbrot bread from the artisanal bakery and ate it in little mouse-bites. No jobs. I organised the bookshelves by genre, the herbs and spices by colour. I went on a brisk jog in the park (avoiding the playground) and hated it. No sleep that night, no sex, no job. I found the cervical-screening letter my father had given me at the casual brunch all those weeks ago, hidden deep in my coat pocket, but decided it was for another day. No job. Saturday: Paul took me to IKEA and let me run around, then made me do YouTube yoga before bed to unwind my hostile mind. No job. On the third day, a sprightly email pinged into my inbox: an interview for a roller-disco hall operating in the old factory part of the city. It felt correct. I spent all afternoon in the overpriced vintage warehouse picking out my bell-bottoms. Paul was very supportive, wishing me good luck while I made my packed lunch the night before. He could be sweet like that. He also didn't say anything the next morning when he saw my new shag haircut that I snipped myself at midnight while he was sleeping, courtesy of an excellent YouTube tutorial. I looked like Stevie Nicks as I got on the bus into town and felt far too sexy to be there. Beads of rain coagulated over the glass of the window, frozen in time over my sultry, sexy reflection. I decided my eyes were everything, my best feature. Smoky. I walked powerfully and with excellent (yet casual) posture to the old factory warehouse turned roller-disco bar — gentrification at its finest. I'd later learn that my grandmother used to work as a jelly-puller in the old custard factory. The place was inviting but intimidating, but that didn't matter because I was cool. However, the fantasy got slightly too enticing. When I got inside and shook hands with the manager, I accidentally spoke in a (surprisingly convincing) American accent (Des Moines' influence?) which I slowly had to transition out of throughout the interview. He almost definitely didn't notice. I was offered a trial shift: Do you roller-skate? he asked. No. Don't worry babe — I'll teach you. He flashed me a smile (literally, cuz he had grillz) and I was escorted to the rink with a pair of size sixes. Within twenty minutes I was a natural; within forty minutes I was a genius. The DJ smiled down at me from on high in the booth on the raised stage and I felt as if I'd won an audience with Zeus. I was a simple servant, a lowly but beautiful mortal offering elegance and grace on wheels. Someone was going to tell a story about me while sculpting pottery or gilding metal, or whatever the modern equivalent was. When the venue opened properly and the punters came in, I had to stop skating and start serving behind the bar, which, incidentally, I'd forgotten to tell the manager that I'd never done before. The manager didn't show me how to use the till either and just gave me his code: You've used one before, right? It's probably the same as your last place. Fortunately, due to the exertion of skating, no one was really interested in drinking anything but tap water. I passed the time cleaning the bar from top to bottom as meticulously as I could and then copied what I'd seen bartenders doing in movies and American sitcoms by looking busy wiping clean things. I perfected my casual: Would you like ice? Nobody noticed I was an imposter. In my careful observations I noticed lots of nose piercings and tattoos and made a mental note to acquire something to help me blend in with my target demographic even further. The place wasn't nearly as 70s as I'd assumed — it was more hip-hop.

No matter. I was fine. I was good. I was peaceful. An hour passed: I was bored. Nobody really needed me. I was a glorified watercooler, that's what my career had come to. (Career?) The branches of people winding round and round the disco floor, once as soothing as a school of fish, had become an affront on my Zen. It was the view from the edge of the school playground again and people were clumped in groups of friends and lovers. Occasionally somebody would get too enthusiastic and fall and I would laugh quietly as they hobbled to the side to nurse their coccyx, but this was not enough to break the monotony. Still, the manager was clearly enamoured with me for organising the stockroom and hyper-cleaning the bar. (Do you have OCD or something? No, I said. He raised his eyebrows: Hey, I'm not complaining!) With no real reason to refuse that I could properly articulate, I accepted the job. Paul was happy for me and took me out for Chinese hotpot to celebrate before the real work began: consistency. That night, after the sex, I took my naked body to the studio one last time, to the sketch of me that she drew, to look at myself; not in the mirror, but in the art. To let it go. The tableau was poignant:

Cleaner

this sketch I couldn't stop thinking about beside an industrial crate of rotting fruit from the market that I'd forgotten about. I stood there for ten minutes or so, staring, the lamplight casting my naked shadow on the wall, and it felt like there were three of me there. My shadow looking at me looking at my image. Eerie. Glum, I trailed to the kitchen and tried to glamorise putting shit white bread in the toaster for a midnight snack. (A woman can't move through a kitchen without it being political or profound — especially naked.) I went through the motions of my traditional housewife parody routine, fondling the fridge door and the bread board and the butter knife, until the toaster popped and I jumped reluctantly into the realisation that if I wasn't an artist, then I was a kept woman, even if I was doing wifely things, ironically. The thought made me hunch over the worktop, buttering in my true form for a moment. A white-spined woman-creature. But the toast was delicious enough to give me sexy posture again. After my fourth piece, it got so cold that it felt like my nipples could cut glass so I returned to Paul and slept soundly. The next morning, I threw out the fruit because I was never going to paint it, because why would I? On paper things seemed to be looking up. My days became identical, indistinguishable from one to the next like a movie montage. It was over a month of waking up at noon, eating a salted pretzel on the walk to the bus, getting on the bus, getting off the bus, walking to the refurbished factory, signing in, stacking and Febrezing stinky roller skates, restocking the bar, de-sticking the ice machine, mopping the floor, watching the regular people skate before the influencers arrived, watching the influencers film themselves pretending to skate before the drunk people arrived, watching the drunk people skate until midnight, closing the bar, waiting for the last bus alone in the empty urban hellscape, getting the last bus home, finding Paul snoring in the bed, staring at the ceiling, falling asleep. Reality. I was consistent and things were better on paper, even if I still felt withered and bereft. The passage of time became marked in the unlikely calendar of mosquitoes squashed against the bedroom wall that I didn't have the heart to remove. In the night they would whine in my ear as if they were trying to tell me something. But consistency made it easier to accept that Isabella wasn't coming back.

Cleaner

I was living with it, and living in her last known address, which was the best place for her to find me again, should she so choose. It was up to her; I'd let it go. At my most deluded, the dusty part of my brain hoped that I'd invented her in a girly *Fight Club* way so that she wasn't gone from me at all and never was; that all I needed to do was get crazier or do something reckless to summon her like Bella in *Twilight: New Moon*, but I knew that was stupid — there was a framed photo of her and Paul from their uni days safely ensconced in the bottom of the chest of drawers, because she was a real person who didn't want me. She was just gone. I was living with it. Paul never complained about me and my parents were leaving me alone, apart from the incessant grandchild updates they shared on the family WhatsApp: blurry mugshots of Des Moines posed like a squashed bowling ball by the fireplace captioned *baby is now the size of a turnip!* I was eating fruit and vegetables regularly again and watching Oscar-bait films on my evenings off. One afternoon, I awoke and saw the tree outside the bedroom window had exonerated its greenness in favour of pale yellow. I realised this was it. There were no tears. I got out of bed, dressed my body in my branded roller-disco T-shirt and bell-bottoms, and headed into work. On my way through town, I took my usual self-indulgent sex-appeal glance at my reflection in my favourite shiny shop window and realised I'd been using a genuinely cool, queer gallery as a mirror this whole time. It stopped me dead. In the window, I looked past the 2D image of a standard woman with a boyfriend, saw the art beyond the glass and wondered whether I'd been practising heterosexuality a little too close to the sun. Is a lifestyle a choice, a costume or the stuff you've been conditioned to do on autopilot? The changing of the seasons should have been a sign. I've often thought of myself as a witch or an idiot: either I notice change and change emerges at my beckoning, or change is constantly waiting for me to notice before it can start. I arrived at work, threw down my tote bag in the cloakroom and started cleaning. Things were entirely normal for the majority of the shift: I wiped things with blue-cloth, I served my signature crispy cold water on the rocks in plastic cups, and stared into space. At halftime I ate my sad, squashed clementine on my twenty-minute break

Cleaner

in the staffroom, and advised a colleague about gaslighting after her boyfriend reportedly blamed his anger issues on her — to her chagrin. I realised too late that she was looking for support and not solutions. Break over, I quietly retreated to complete my toilet checks and added in a few missing apostrophes onto some fresh graffiti scribbled by the sanitary bin. We were a lot busier than usual — that was the only negligible indicator of disruption. Behind the bar again, my manager had checked in on how I was doing in an uncharacteristic expression of responsibility: You good? We were half an hour away from midnight when the music seemed to puncture the air in a way that spiked my eardrums. The crowd spiralled faster, pushing themselves, and I could no longer zone out — a large crowd of new arrivals, loud and brutish, glided in on their skates and were assimilating into the crowd. The place felt full of men. As I say, we were busier than normal and at maximum capacity; people were drunk and shouting over the music, clutching their friends in the cyclone. Something seemed to be kicking off in the centre of the dancefloor; nothing out of the ordinary, but always a concern. On the sidelines, people were meerkatting to see the ruckus. Security would pick it up in a second. One man was squaring (rolling) up to another with intent. I pinched the loose skin of my elbow hard to jolt some sense into my brain. Then, suddenly, I saw and understood what was disquieting me. A particular figure meandering through the punters was too familiar. The hair, the musculature of the back. The sleek hair. I was so sure it was her (in a white ABBA jumpsuit that was somehow messianic). I vaulted over the bar and made for the dancefloor. Like in a film, I saw everything in a sluggish, hypersaturated fashion; the grimaces and pouts of the customers as I pushed to get to her; the slosh of a cup of ice water; my manager from the sidelines mouthing: What the fuck? I forgot he didn't know Isabella: LOOK! I yelled, pointing into the mob of people where she was supposed to be. But something had happened in the split second I'd turned away: the image had changed from divinity to horror. She had disappeared and, in the fight, like a poem, I caught the twinkling of the blade first before the jab into the unsuspecting abdomen. Not mine, just some poor bloke who was in the wrong place at the wrong time. His scream was the first scream. Then it was his girlfriend's. Then it was mine. I can't really recall what happened next. After the house lights were switched on and the ambulance had arrived and the police tape was set up, I found myself behind the bar again, pouring shaky cups of water for the initial response team. Thanks, love. No problem. One curly-haired paramedic stayed at the bar for a moment, sipping, and we stared in companionable silence at the blood pooled on the dancefloor. The body was being dealt with by his colleagues. They were debating whether this was easier or harder than their previous call. The cardiac arrest in the bathtub. Trying to lift him out. Dropped him. Big wet corpse. I turned to the curly-haired one. It felt like the wrong time to ask, but I thought I'd never get another opportunity: Is it always this weird? His fish-hook smile whispered *yes*. I wondered if creepy algorithm social media and the news and horror movies had desensitised me to what I had just witnessed/what I was witnessing. Blood just looked like gratuitous fake blood or blood on the news, therefore I couldn't see it for what it was. Like when I finally saw the Mona Lisa in the flesh on a school trip and realised it was exactly what I had expected, only A4. Has modernity diluted the aesthetic of death? I could look at the warm blood on the floor but I could not perceive. When a group of freshers tried to barge their way back in to film the sinister content, I basically rugby-tackled them out of eyeline like one of those poor, exploited, social-media content moderators, just without the prism of the screen. It was just another day at the office; the blood was no less ordinary than a spilled drink. Caution: Wet Floor. Then I saw a flash of the portrait of the dead man on the stupid fresher's phone screen; his face poking out from the body bag he was being swaddled in by the paramedics like a dead baby, the zip just reaching his chin in the still of the photo, and I was hit with a wave of delayed nausea. This was the second murder I'd been proximal to. What was I being told? Somebody's baby was dead. And his girlfriend, I'd heard her screaming. My manager bumbled over on autopilot with the look of death about him, sweat pixelling his forehead: You can go home now, good work today. I didn't need telling twice. I grabbed my tote bag from the staffroom and slid out the fire exit. The wind stabbed my face as I walked and I tried very hard not to think about knives disappearing into flesh or people panicking and screaming and falling and scrambling. It was only when I was at the stop, waiting for the last bus, that I remembered the perpetrator(s) were still at large — but there was no one behind me. Standing alone by the bus stop on the long, barren street within the bricked-up labyrinth of the city underbelly, under the vast, black sky, I felt no more scared than usual. I had one of my moments of cold profundity, where I acknowledged that behind every half-open warehouse door, past every white van, between every alley, around every corner there was going to be a murdering rapist thief — or there wasn't. I was going to be on the street anyway. The geometric sci-fi moon seemed to rear its pointy chin at me in solidarity. Stoicism. Out of nowhere, a sports car sped past and fired a firework out of the passenger side window, skimming the top of my head before smacking into the brick wall behind. A man's laughter wailed away as more fireworks popped into the night. I was too stunned to cry. The streetlamp I was standing next to seemed to lean over me protectively and I sidled under its wing out of the darkness. Under the light, I imagined myself suspended like a prehistoric fly cast in amber and I wished so badly for it to be true, that I was a fly from a bygone era that had just stopped for a moment on a tree, drawn to the taste of something different, only to realise with a smile that this was it; the world was caving in and I was to be kept safe in the orange forever and ever. But the bus came. I stepped out of the light and onto the street again. Back in the flat, Paul's body was warm in the bed and I latched myself to the steady rumble of it. No sleep. The dawn chorus was sombre and I shook with anxiety at the recollection that death comes in threes. When Paul woke and asked what time I was leaving for work the next day, I told him I wasn't. Showed him a fresh news article on the roller-disco murderer on my phone. He understood. While he scrolled on his iPad, I gnashed my teeth over the skin and nail of my thumb, pulled purple from years of cannibalising myself. It was Saturday. Paul scrunched his face: Don't bite. I looked him in the eye. Or what? What he said next surprised me: Would you like me to sit for you? I was perplexed: Pardon? He reiterated, gently: Would you like me to sit for you? He led me to the studio, made me undress him, piece by piece, until he was clean and empty and waiting. He said: Where do you want me? The breeze from the open window coaxed beautiful goosebumps from his skin. I sat him on a stool and propped him into the curved, meaningful slouch of someone paying attention while you're talking. It was so much easier to paint when it wasn't just from my imagination. I painted for hours and hours. He asked me all sorts of questions, questions that I answered because I wanted to answer, about my art and my brain. It was fun to puddle paint onto canvas again: I luxuriated in vivid jade, azure, and hallucinatory rose. After a while, the foregrounded image of the painted Paul blended with the human Paul and they seemed to open their mouths together as uncanny doubles, or as a puppet and master, I wasn't quite sure. Paul: Can I see it? He crept cartoonishly round the easel, fixed his gaze on his likeness. He didn't speak for a moment. It hadn't crossed my mind until that point that he might be offended by my depiction of him. He spoke: You've painted me... very well. The smile on his face was unreadable. But he cupped my chin in his hand and kissed me softly, lowered me to the floor. The sex felt different. The painted Paul, exorcised from his body, watched us intently from above with the interested posture I'd given him. Look at *me*, he said. And I came. Afterwards, Paul left to go and watch the rugby in the pub, while I stayed to add the finishing touches. As much as I hated to admit it, the painting seemed a lot less successful after my orgasm. I put it aside and resolved to start afresh tomorrow — at least I was back into the swing of things. Now that I was creating again, the unfinished playground project felt as if it deserved my attention first. Conceding that Paul was right and that crochet was in fact a silly idea grounded in my own narcissism, I ransacked B&Q and waited patiently for nightfall. The art, this time, was for them. Paint pots in hand and rollers stowed in the suitcase, I careered up the hill without thinking to check for witnesses; when I opened the gate to the playground, I was met with the luminous, animal stare of the hoodied teenagers glancing up from their phones. I shuddered: Excuse me, sorry, is it okay if I start painting? No answer. They seemed struck dumb at the prospect of my invading their dominion. However, I felt their silence didn't mean no. With professional speed and a

Cleaner

fake-it-till-you-make-it attitude, I set up my station and started splashing pure white paint strategically over the gaudy plastic; Paul would be back from the pub soon and I had no time to feel self-conscious. I needn't have worried. The youths were indifferent to my daubing — or so I thought. After around ten minutes, I was approached by the tallest one, because it looked kind of fun and basically, yeah, he liked painting, and could he and his boys get involved in your thing. Sure, no problem, I said. Grab yourself a brush. The group effort minimised the workload dramatically. Within the hour, the obnoxious colour-vomit plastic had become a snow-white palace of imaginative purity. A fresh start. I looked around at my new colleagues: You've each done a good thing today. I shook each of their hands in turn and wished them all the best in their future careers and lives. They would never see me again, I would just be a memory. A paint ghost. I wheeled down the hill with a paint-splattered suitcase and a head full of dreams. Perhaps they would grow old and grey with hoodied offspring of their own and tell the story of this night. I turned around for one more look and was rewarded with the sight of a playground glowing under the eye of the full moon. A fortress of childhood protected. Tomorrow, when the goalkeeper mums wheeled the children in, they would have a blank canvas to graffiti, paint, crayon, go wherever their intuition took them. The playground was theirs again and not what grown-ups thought they needed. Their habitat had been decolonised. In the distance, the hoodied shadows waved goodbye and touched my soul. Giving is a wonderful thing. I disposed of the ruined suitcase in a wheelie bin and was back at the flat in time to greet a mellow, effusive Paul, who wanted to recount the match he watched in triplicate. I wrapped him up in his bed and kissed his forehead to bless the image; he was a boy again in sleep and I was truly the custodian of childhood dreams. This privilege came with a cost. In payment, sleep placed me in the school playground of my own youth with the friendships I couldn't grow. In my dream, I chased a girl I desperately wanted to befriend in a large figure of eight while the others watched in assessment, ready to grade me on some criteria I wasn't privy to. The more she ran away from me, the more I pursued, until I realised she had disappeared and I was running in circles after no one. The girls from my childhood spoke in chorus: we did a test just then. You're following so-and-so around all the time and copying everything she does — but she's not your friend. Why are you crying? You're so sensitive... I sweated awake, only dimly aware of a nightmare. It was still too early to get up, so I stared at the ceiling and tried to quantify how mad Paul would get if I painted it, Sistine-style. Whether the risk was worth the reward. I was still pondering the pros and cons hours later when Paul barged into the kitchen. He was frothing at the mouth and I was rolling out instant filo pastry for a Mediterranean vegetable tart: Was this you? He held up his phone. On the screen there was a pretty heated post in the local Facebook group about the beloved children's playground being 'vandalised' (a pretty loaded word, I thought, with disturbing connotations). The comments streamed down in a big river of online outrage: *Why would someone do this? Is this some kind of practical joke?* Paul's eyes were twitching and his mouth was open in a little cherry pout. *How am I going to explain this to my kids?* I scrolled down further, taking my time. Comments were flocking in, listing theories about whether the paint was a protest for something, or whether it was an emergency anti-graffiti initiative from the council — in which case, the money would be better spent on the NHS. One comment wondered whether it was a memorial of some kind, the playground being white and all (clicking on the commenter's profile, I recognised The Goalkeeper Mum I had spoken to and instantly felt rumbled). *Some disturbed nutter trying to make a point.* I smiled to myself and knew it was just the initial shock; once the drama died down, things would recalibrate into a new and improved normal. Paul tutted: Well? I didn't answer. Paul rightly assumed my silence didn't mean no. He expressed disappointment. I questioned why he was disappointed. He was not able to provide a clear answer. An hour later we ate the Mediterranean tart with a dressed side salad and got over the impasse quite nicely. Having uncorked my buried talent, I began painting ceaselessly and with the kind of boundless energy artists only seem to have in biographies or history documentaries. Everything was inspirational: the bin, the Nespresso, the radiator, the three toothbrushes lolling away from each other in the holder. I painted everything

Cleaner

and ate everything in sight in random charcuterie style. French bread, mandarins, Babybels. Brushing my teeth one morning, I dislodged some corner of my gum and spat blood into the sink. In the berry spots on the white ceramic, I divined perhaps my most pithy project yet: what to do with the erotica man's manuscript. It was so simple and yet so symbolic to dig it out of my inbox, print it out in its entirety using Paul's printer in the office (post-spellcheck, of course) and dissect the narrative with scissors. Unsexy sexy words fluttered in little paper rectangles onto the studio floor for me to scramble and re-order accordingly. It made the most sense to glue them to canvas starting on the edges and then spiralling inwards like a snail shell; a vortex of degradation made cleaner. Over his words and my arrangement of them, I used watercolour to paint the scene of the two of us sitting at that edgy bar all those months ago; his moon-crater face animated in what was likely his last day of storytelling and the back of my head and shoulders tilted in reaction. It dried almost instantaneously in a puff of magic. I was proud of my (our) work. This denouement invited further reflections on the art I was custodian of, not all of them welcome. The headless nude portrait of me that Isabella left on the easel all those months ago had been calling out in the night for something. I'd walk past the closed studio door and it would wail, despondent, bottomless. Ignoring it was essential. It would be satanic to separate the loyalty of my heart from my professional eye; her drawing was sacred and I could not touch it, even if it needed a little shading here and there. Falling in love with painting again sparked an uncomfortable hunch in the recesses of my mind. I'd always assumed that Isabella had cleared her studio before she left the flat (presumably to keep her soul distant from mine) but, the more I thought about it, the more I wondered whether there was all that much to clear. The studio wasn't bare so much as barren. So where was all her art? Lying in bed one night, the wailing became an uncanny tinnitus. I tossed and turned but nothing soothed it. Asking it to be quiet made no difference, it could not understand me. In my psychosis, I knew rather than felt the wailing travel from the studio to the inside of the bedroom, pouring under the gap in the door and drifting under the bed. Feverishly, I jumped out of the duvet to follow it — there was nothing there, and I knew this because I vacuumed under the bed regularly. So what was I hearing? Paul had left the window open and the breeze blustered intently through the blinds, accentuating the phantasmagoria. I was hearing something else. With the strength of a gym bro, I lifted the double mattress off the bedframe and was rewarded with the sight of a medium black sketchbook tucked atop the slats. Buried treasure! The wailing seemed to swell into visceral groans in the air, filling the room with an unearthly chorus, but then I realised it was just Paul, confused and rolling down the bed: hngghhhh... what's going on? I grabbed the sketchbook and dropped the mattress with a thump, ran away to the studio, and illuminated it under the desk lamp. This was her work! I smoothed the first page open carefully; a skyline of New York. Basic, but not without promise. The next page was blank. The following page was another sunset skyline of a nondescript city in oil pastels. Again, inoffensive. And that was it. The rest of the pages were covered sparsely in ballpoint sketches of bits and bobs. Her subjects varied little; there was more than one scribble of a squashed-nose pug, undoubtedly created via a cute

YouTube tutorial. This was the artistic equivalent of a Pinterest board. I sat upright, slapping the sketchbook closed. A long and pointy truth licked down the inside of my ear canal and into my brain, unwelcome, necessary; her soul wasn't in her art. It didn't matter if she was an artist; her soul wasn't here. So where was it? Her spiritual self-portrait had to be somewhere. I looked through her work again, determined to see something different, but knowing in my heart that there was nothing new to see. Everything she had drawn had so obviously been done before. Was she trying to hide behind other people's work? Or, worse, was she even aware that she was hiding? This question moved me to reflect upon the transparency of my own creations. I, the artist, did not appear much as a figure in my work, save for a handful of notable exceptions: the meeting with The Erotica Man with the word-scramble of his work surrounding, of course; a portrait composite of mine and Isabella's faces, a hybrid rendering of our bodies staring intently at the viewer, hands folded gently, unknowable smile on her face; the swaddled baby corpse of the roller-rink victim lying alone on the floor, with me serving water sweatily at the bar

Cleaner

(there's nothing quite like other people's suffering — how much death does it take for me to pick up my paintbrush? The perfect dose to put me in the productivity sweet spot?) There was also the triptych of a dinner-party scene in the flat, with the first depicting me in the kitchen prepping vegetables and deboning fish, the second depicting Isabella hosting like a Roman emperor (my distorted reflection relegated to a metal serving bowl), and the final depicting the clean-up the next morning, where I'm on my hands and knees amongst the food waste and Isabella is stroking my hair. Paul featured fairly frequently in twiny, wiry flourishes to a domestic scene, but mostly the world appeared in objects and colours. Paul said one evening: These aren't bad, you know. I smiled: *I know*. He twirled the spaghetti I made him round his fork thoughtfully. I have something to ask you, he said. He put down his plate, got down on one knee in front of me, took the weight of my hands in his, and pulled me close: why don't you start an Instagram account? For your art? With the right marketing strategy, you could probably make some decent money, you know. How long has it been since you left the roller-skating place now?

The corners of his mouth were stained orange from the pasta sauce and I wondered if I could re-create it on canvas: Don't move! I yelled, and ran away. When I came back, I could see he had moved, even though he'd clearly tried very hard not to, which infuriated me. Never mind! Paul hid in the office for the rest of the evening. I was later punished for my impudence with a burgeoning stye that I could feel burning and sprouting under my top eyelid. The more I poked it, the more I felt like one of those lab rats that can't stop pushing their suicide button. Of course, the next morning it was swollen and pink and painful, with a burst blood vessel casting a lightning streak under my skin. I painted it in the cool light of the morning as penance. Once again, the visual trinity mystified me: me staring at my eye with the stye in the hand mirror, the eye with the stye within the hand mirror staring at me, me painting my eye with the stye on the canvas, the eye with the stye within the canvas staring at me, each eye with the stye staring and sizing each other up accordingly. Ugly, yet profound. The pharmacy gave me a tube of antibiotic grease to squeeze under my eyelid but I didn't apply it as directed as it made my vision blurry. It threw my perspective totally off. The stye looked pleased with itself. Over the course of the week, it bloomed yellow and triumphant. Paul took to looking at it when he spoke to me about finances and my needing to find another job, as if the stye needed to start paying rent too. Our first proper fight. I took a sulky walk to the local function room to partake in a clinical or consumer trial or something I saw advertised on Google. That's not a job though, is it! But it was £20 to eat an ice-cream and answer a questionnaire about my wellbeing. There was a handwritten sign pasted to the window outside the place: EAT ICE-CREAM FOR CASH! COME INSIDE. (ADULTS ONLY). The face of a grey-haired, wolfish woman peered at me through the window and smiled, beckoned me in with her finger. I was given a clipboard and escorted into a dim, empty room with a leather sofa and an ugly Wetherspoons-type carpet. There was a TV buzzing a random history programme on one of those trolleys used in schools before interactive whiteboards. I stood expectantly in the centre of the room. She stood opposite. We stood there. Then I asked about the ice-cream. Mmmmm… she moaned in a theatrical fashion and handed me a Cornetto, pinched a smile on her face: It's delicious. I'll leave you to it! The questionnaire started out simply enough. Name, address, nationality, gender, sexuality. On a scale of 1–10, how would you describe your sugar consumption? On a scale of 1–10, how calm would you say you are currently? Would you describe your ice-cream intake as a) rare b) sometimes c) frequent d) regular? On a scale of 1–10, how would you rate the ice-cream you are currently eating? How happy are you right now on a scale of 1–10? The TV was playing WWII documentary footage for some reason. How happy are you right now on a scale of 1–10? Right now. I took my first lick of the ice-cream and realised I was in a neoliberal nightmare. What's the most you would pay for this ice-cream a) £0.99 b) £1.99 c) £2.50 d) £2.99)? The door to the room was half-open but I was trapped. I was in a village hall eating an ice-cream with a survey to justify someone's professional development portfolio in a meeting about assets and growth. The wolfish woman heard or smelled my thoughts and came shuffling back into the room to lick my fur and coddle me into another demeaning quiz to wring me of market potential. In a fit of rage at my professional impotency, I speared the ice-cream onto her nose and made a break for it. And break I did. I stormed and raged through the street, scaring a teen mum and a child in a buggy, and kicking a bin and hurting my toe. Ashamed, I hobbled back to the flat and crashed into Paul on the landing: How did it go? I didn't get the money. What do you mean you didn't get the money? I didn't finish it. What do you mean you didn't finish it, it was a fucking survey? We argued for around ten minutes before I left again. I wandered down to the canal to look at the floating dead fish and remember life could be worse. Life could be a lot worse. Their oily droplet eyes were a bad omen. When I got back to the flat, Paul asked me to leave. He was sorry but he just needed some space to think things through, he said, with the custard face of an Education Minister explaining something obvious to a child on *Newsround*. Where had this come from? I packed a rucksack full of Isabella's clothes and stared at him in the hallway: You can come collect your paintings from the studio later. Okay. This isn't goodbye, he said to the stye. Okay.

You're a really nice person, I just… He had the face of everyone I ever knew. It made me smile, in spite of everything. Back on the street, the heat was cloying and annoying and I couldn't bear to look at all the happy, well-adjusted people going home from work to their families. Disassociating for ease of movement, my attention was caught for a moment walking through the inner city, peeking through the masonic houses at the Aston Martins cooped inside car-park bunkers. I knew I was, rather than felt myself to be, upset, which I supposed to be a small gift of self-preservation given by a bemused, low-ranking god. In the park, I went to the playground, expecting to find some degree of solace and validation but was instead faced with more failure. The playground was empty of children; a gaunt scaffold of unrealised potential. No attempt had been made to interact with my public art — apart from a lone swastika scribbled on the climbing frame, which didn't count. Why weren't the children here? They had a blank canvas! I checked online and was immediately crushed. Fears over the toxicity of the paint had spread on the local Facebook community group and no doubt the goalkeeper mums' WhatsApp too.

Cleaner

Reams of comments, cutting comments: *Not taking my child back until it's safe. No longer feel safe bringing my kids here — such a shame as had been coming for years. I'm not exposing my child to toxic poison! #boycottthepark.* The council had been tagged fifty times with demands to fix the problem immediately and why hadn't they fixed the problem immediately and where is my taxpayer money going exactly? I imagined the children confined to their living rooms fighting over the family iPad and realised I had, in essence, achieved the exact opposite of what I set out to do. I was the imagination killer; a bubo in the armpit of society. Sat on a park bench, I watched a bumblebee curl up and die on the hot concrete — an awful place to whine its end. It didn't occur to me to do something about it until it was still and silent. The guilt didn't come but I stood vigil until I felt enough courage to face my parents' house again. They didn't seem surprised at my return or the fact that my eyelid was pus-yellow and tripled in size. My father was on the computer with his noise-cancelling headphones on and merely nodded in my direction. No kiss, no hug, no questions. My mother had hurt her back and was more verbose in her greeting — she was hopeful I was 'having one of my moments' and would clean the oven for her with my perfectionist tendencies. Activated like a sleeper agent, I immediately ran upstairs and slammed my bedroom door teenage-style. Hello? Nestled under my duvet was a woman of about forty with dark hair tied carelessly into a top-knot. She was polite and spoke with an Eastern European accent: Can I help you? I ran back downstairs to my mother, who reminded me that we were doing our bit as a family for the war effort, flicking a tea towel over her shoulder and flexing her biceps like she was one of the ammunition girls. Homes for Ukraine — We talked about this! Tatiana made Vareniki for dinner and I sulked at the end of the dining table and said nothing, feeling guilty about the bee. When my mother suggested watching a film 'as a family', I hid in the bathroom and squeezed the stye until it popped. The release of tension was instantaneous and orgasmic. I smiled shyly at my reflection and felt for the first time in a long time that everything was going to be okay, looking myself in the eye. Then I remembered I was alive and that behind my skin was a skull and electric jelly, and that instead

Cleaner

of my skeleton being inside of me, I was inside of my skeleton. It threw me beyond language. Panicked and unable to feel my hands properly, I squashed myself between my mother and Tatiana on the sofa to watch *The Death of Stalin* (Dad's choice) until it was time for bed. Relegated to the sofa with a blanket for the foreseeable, I was forced to listen to the living-room clock tick all night long. When I was finally free, sleep pinched me awake too early to acknowledge the dawn over the garden — the silhouette of the tree pointing at morning in a disco pose. Being back at my parents' house in the shadow of their new Ukrainian ward brought subconscious agonies to the shore of my brain. When my mother commented on Tatiana's beautiful head of hair, I became hyper-aware of some minor pattern hair loss I was experiencing, which led to an hour-long examination of the back of my head in the mirror, which led to a complex on how flat the back of my head was, which led to a misguided fantasy of wanting to pop my skull round again like a misshapen ping-pong ball. Tatiana's no trouble, is she? Really self-sufficient. Did you know Tatiana is still running her travel agency remotely, despite having to flee a warzone? My mortification was extreme. I occupied most of my time healing my eye with hot compresses and completing jigsaws of the Pre-Raphaelites: *The Lady of Shalott*, *Ophelia*, *Isabella and The Pot of Basil*. On the third day of my return, my mother manipulated the two of us into attending a body-combat session with her — myself, because I 'had to do *something* today', and Tatiana because she didn't have the language to refuse politely. Mum directed her most matronly *Call the Midwife* voice onto me: What have you done today to keep yourself occupied? (I'd read an article about how the melting ice caps were destabilising gravity and making the Earth wobble and my mother had witnessed my ensuing meltdown by the washing machine with vexation.) We arrived at the leisure centre in the early evening. When the security guards nodded at me, my mother whispered loudly about maybe getting my job as the pool cleaner back, which I ignored. We queued politely outside the studio with the other mums and waited. Tatiana seemed unimpressed with the floury pudginess of the English figure as she stretched and wound her ankles in circles. I consoled myself that my mother's spare Lycra at least sat loosely on me. During my earlier tantrum by the washing machine, I'd knocked my forearm into the door handle and a little plum bruise had formed — minuscule, insignificant. I would have remained unaware of this, had my mother not seen fit to prod it sharply with her finger (You've got a bruise there!) and I couldn't work out if this was a conscious or an unconscious attempt to motivate me to punch things. The door was opened by a small woman, who ushered us all in with her impressive muscular arms and thick French accent. I sat with my water bottle on the bench and avoided my reflection on the mirrored wall, paid on the card machine with my own money, even though Mum had said she was going to. Where were the punching bags for body combat? What were we combatting? The instructor started her bass-heavy playlist and began jumping and punching the air to the beat, sparring with nothing. I was out of breath immediately. Tatiana took herself into the front row while I retreated to the back row and tried unsuccessfully to return the sinking gusset of my mother's leggings to my crotch. Copying the routine was more difficult than I expected and I crashed into her more times than was necessary, she felt. The instructor's explicit encouragement directed at me had the opposite effect: I wanted nothing more than to cry or give up or both. Hyah! Cringe. Sweat. Punching the air in front of my reflection felt redundant — I wasn't sure who or what I was supposed to be punching. However, my shame eventually morphed into indifference. I became entranced by the gurning faces of all the women, including my own, punching and kicking imaginary obstacles. Maybe I would paint them. Tatiana looked particularly invested and I wondered what she saw in the space between her fist and her reflection. My mother locked eyes with me — I didn't want to know. By the end of the session, I was trembling and weak. The instructor changed the music to a power ballad and spoke with such gentleness during the cooldown that I fell asleep on the yoga mat. I laughed it off with the other women. It wasn't endorphins exactly, but it was something. Nothing was said in the car ride home but I could feel something brewing in my mother as I sat in the back seat watching the trees blur by through the window. After Tatiana took herself off to my room, she waited by the microwave with a probiotic yoghurt: Have you booked your smear test yet? No. Do you want to get cervical cancer and die? Yes. She laughed and shook her head like I'd said something funny. I got cocky: You can't send me to my room, there's a Ukrainian there. No, I can't — grow up. An ambulance wailed by on the street and we waited for the moment to pass. She made her move for the living room and I made for the bottom of the garden, wishing I had the excuse of being a smoker. I checked my phone; Paul and I sexted for a while until he wanted pictures and I realised I couldn't strip off, let alone masturbate in my parents' garden, where I'd played as a child. The rusty scaffold of the slide my dad had erected in my youth moved me to review the nature of time and memory. I realised, properly for the first time, that my bare feet were a product of evolution and I was just another fucking monkey — my enclosure was just too small and understimulating. Bored of imagining sex with Paul, my thoughts drifted through known human history, reassured that in the past I'd have been very good at whatever occupation I'd have inherited from my parents. Awakened, my ancestral spirit longed for that mundane, repetitive task of digging or weaving or carving that was essential for the survival of the tribe; braving the battle of each season as they came. Images of myself fighting against wind and snow, clutching runes or tribal jewellery sacred to the community preoccupied me — then it got a bit cold and I thought about going inside again. Above in my bedroom window, I watched the dark shadow of Tatiana pace back and forth on the phone, crying or laughing to someone far away. The next morning, I rang the GP and got a same-day appointment. My mother was smug: Do you want me to talk you through it? I ran away before she could give me any advice, suffocated by the wrong kind of attention. I didn't want to be patronised, I didn't want goal-keeping. I wanted to be asked how I was feeling and I wanted to sleep in my own bed. The walk to the surgery was shorter than I remembered and I ended up completing three circuits of the high street, clocking my reflection in shop windows, before flopping down in a seat in the waiting room. The clinical smell and the infographics about STDs and domestic abuse pinned to the cork boards made me anxious. A grey and exhausted mother with a small, snotty child and another rounding belly stared at me as I bounced my leg up and down. We both diligently scrolled on our phones to avoid speaking to each other. I watched at least twenty reels of conservative American wives packing elaborate lunches for their husbands heading out to work, hating myself for drooling over their fucking illusion and their fucking agas. When the snotty boy ran off to the far corner of the room, he seemed to forget who he belonged to. After tripping over nothing, he wailed, ran back, and imprinted his wet face upon my knee. Compelled by robotic maternal instinct, I cupped his head in the palm of my hand and soothed him for some minutes. I was the village. The mother and I said nothing about it. The boy wouldn't let go of my ankle until I was called in by the nurse. She led me into the little side room and talked cheerfully about what was going to happen through a gap-tooth. Something about the texture of her hair and chubbiness of her face reminded me of a middle-aged Orphan Annie: Don't be nervous. I was aware I seemed nervous but I wasn't actually nervous like a normal person. It would have been rational to be nervous in the face of an unknown and slightly invasive procedure. Instead, I was all of a sudden overcome with grief and could hardly listen to what she was saying. Where had all the time gone? Surely I wasn't old enough for this yet? There had been another cheerful nurse once, administering my HPV vaccine, who'd foreshadowed the smear when I was a girl in secondary school. It had all felt so far away. Small pinch. Well done. After the Orphan Annie nurse explained what was to happen, I was led behind the blue curtain to the examining table. I blinked back the tears as I took my pants off, lay down and spread my legs like a frog under the white paper covering as she instructed. She pulled back the curtain: Are you all right? I was crying. There's nothing to be scared of, I promise. I looked up at her head of curly hair, fanned out in a halo as it eclipsed the lightbulb. Insufficient words dribbled out of the corner of my mouth: I know, it's all just a bit weird. It's all right, love. She inserted the speculum and narrated everything she was doing like a good nurse does. You might feel a little bit of pressure now, small pinch. Well done… then it was over. It was nothing. After I was clothed again, she showed me the little bloody sample in the sterile jar, got me to double-check my date of birth that she'd scrawled

Cleaner

on it in Biro, and explained how I'd get a letter with my results in a few weeks' time. The most time-consuming bit is the paperwork afterwards, she said. Sign your initials here, are you sure you're all right? I smiled and said I was fine, I wasn't going to make a disclosure, I was just that sort of person. She smiled back without pity and I felt the strangest urge to crawl inside her mouth and live in the gap between her teeth; I wanted to drink the purpose in her. With a sincerity bordering on the religious, I thanked the nurse for her kindness and left, revelling in the sensation of nothing having gone wrong. A flock of birds erupted over the horizon and a cool, disinterested voice in my ear told me I could be a nurse if I wanted to. In the Oxfam I found a little blue shift dress with a 'V' neck and white piping that looked the part, especially when I twisted my hair into a low, sleek bun. Surely there was some student funding still available to me? I walked home in my makeshift nurse outfit, smiling out my fantasy, but took it off when I saw my mother's face and my father's indifference. Tatiana was drinking a cup of boiled water and lemon at the dining-room table: So, what do you have job as exactly? I curved the heavy corners of my mouth upwards: I'm a cleaner. Defeated, I rang my old boss at the leisure centre but he wouldn't take me back. The further education college didn't pick up and the estate agency didn't remember I'd worked there at all. My only hope was the art gallery and I wasn't sure I was ready to retread that floor with the vacuum, ringed with symbolism as that place was to me. The place where I'd met that woman. How many months had passed since our first meeting? And how much had changed, really, since then? Empty, I lay back against the sofa cushions and let my mouth hang open, as if I was dead. Instead of moving on, it seemed as though I'd grown around my longing, storing the way she made me feel safely in my belly. I wasn't deluded; I knew I didn't really know her, but I felt sure that she had something to impart, that I was to gain something necessary from her. The vow I'd made to forget her was pointless, it was clear waiting for her return had made no difference; I needed to bring her to me another way. Scrolling through the social-media pages of the gallery — the prosecco bar, the selfie station, the shit nudes drawn by members of the public at the life-drawing classes on Thursday nights — the plan that would create change came to me of its own accord. Upon leaving Paul's flat, an idea had been ruminating in the recesses of my mind for some time but the impetus to tackle such a scheme had eluded me until now. Searching for an affirmative sign, the green light on the Wi-Fi box under the television had to do. I threw myself into the task of organising such a high-wire act. First, I rang Paul to talk about the logistics of transporting my art from the flat studio. He was more enthusiastic than I expected him to be, which added credence to my cause. Equally, the gallery was happy to host my exhibition when I contacted them and, based on the tenor of the emails exchanged, I felt certain the owner had forgotten the circumstances in which we had last crossed paths in the disabled toilet. My confidence wavered a little when I saw how much it would cost to rent the space for the evening but, pitted against the alternative, I knew the purchase was unavoidable. Money would return. One day I would have money. The date was set for a month's time, to give me sufficient time to prepare. After taking a YouTube crash course in Canva, I designed logos and digital art to use as part of my marketing strategy (spamming social media and sticking things to trees and coffee-shop windows). ART EXHIBITION! ONE NIGHT ONLY! I spent the month ordering leaflets from the local print shop and trawling the city to distribute them. There was something vaguely nomadic and mediaeval about the month I spent in the lead-up. It became a pilgrimage of sorts as I spiralled round the outskirts of the suburbs, circling in slowly on the map to the place I knew my journey was to end. The apex of my Bildungsroman: the gallery. Overcome with pre-show jitters the night before, I looked at the place, the bus stop outside, to reassure myself it was still there and that I hadn't dreamt the past up. It was grottier than I remembered it to be, presumably in the absence of a good cleaner, as it stood squinting at me from the top of the high street. Tomorrow would mean something: either the beginning of a new chapter or the continuation of the same. I felt the urge to light a candle like in my Catholic school days, so I went into the corner shop to buy a cheap plastic lighter and stood on the street with the flame. Night had spun down over the world quietly again. In the darkness of the street, under the gaze of a perfect quarter-moon peeking out like a shark's fin over the grey clouds, I was holy in my borrowed windbreaker. Cars raced by on the road in blurs. A puff of wind shocked the flame out and I knew that it was time. This was it. I was brought out of my reverie by the sudden fall of an acorn hitting me on the head with a thump. Fate was clearly nudging me away from the scene, so I'd not reach my destiny too soon. Nodding to the tree in thanks felt like the right thing to do. I sauntered home with the leisure of a dreamer and an artist. As I turned the corner to face my childhood home, however, the sight of my father's shadow in the window brought a disturbance to the air within my lungs. Peripeteia: I felt it in the back of my throat. I don't remember crossing the threshold or my mother whisking me inside, but she placed a cup of tea under my nose and looked at me very seriously with marbled eyes: Des Moines had lost the baby — stillbirth. In the other room I could see the figure of my father moving to sit down quietly at the television, unwilling to talk about it. Tatiana hummed to herself as she stood by the kettle waiting for it to reboil. Of all things, my first thought was that the gender-reveal portrait was cursed after all, that Isabella had granted them an unwitting memento mori. The only visual memory of this almost-child in the consciousness of its parents' acquaintance would be one so comical and untrue as to eclipse the thought of what the real face might've looked like. Ugliness. Until that moment, I'd never thought to imagine what features my nephew might've inherited. I never bothered to look at the ultrasound. All I could see was the unveiling of the ugly portrait and the insincere smiles of the guests at the party, including my own. I despised Isabella's carelessness for the first time. My second thought was for my brother and Des Moines. The rest of the evening passed in respectful solicitude and silence. Our four bodies roamed the borders of the house and changed direction aimlessly and aggressively like snooker balls after the break. There were no dreams that night — my ego was quiet, for once — and the next morning brought nothing with it: no ambition, no excitement. In fact, I wasn't sure whether I wanted to go ahead with the exhibition at all. Getting up from under the warmth of the blanket on the sofa seemed impossible until it felt all too reminiscent of the womb. Eventually, I got up and ate an absent-minded breakfast of white bread and jam, while watching a baleful money spider crawl over a leaf of the cheese plant. Unnervingly, when I stepped out of the shower half an hour later, I found myself eye to eye with a single thread of web dangling from the ceiling, crystallised with condensation. A message perhaps. In the end I dressed like the spider, in all black, to be the artist. Belt, boots, muscle-fit T-shirt. No other costume could have worked this time. When I checked the clock, it was barely 10am — hours before Paul was to deliver my paintings to the gallery. Without anything to do but wait, I slunk back into my anxiety coma and flirted on the edge of ringing him to cancel. The will to go on was entirely lost to me until my father summoned us all into the living room for a 'family meeting', to fill out the census, or rather, to confirm what he had already filled out for us on the computer. We lined up in an orderly fashion to review our information: Name, address, nationality, occupation, gender, sexuality. Can *I* put it into the computer, please? No, just tell me. Wouldn't it be faster if I did it myself? Why, have you got somewhere to be? After he read out all of my identity information correctly, apart from my sexuality, I was forced to come out to my parents and Tatiana. No one said anything. I guess I could have lied, but I didn't. I waited. My mother sneezed obnoxiously, asking where my father had put the box of tissues, and I questioned whether pure, uncut indifference was in fact homophobic or progressive. I waited a little longer but no one had anything to say. My dad moved the mouse to unclick 'heterosexual' and click the correct box. I waited until I could wait no longer and spoke in the biggest voice I could manage: Okay, I'll see you at the gallery later then. My father: What time does it start? 7pm. Okay, is there going to be alcohol at this thing? Yes, there's going to be alcohol at my *solo exhibition* in a *professional art gallery*. It's a celebration, why? Well, don't drink too much. I told him with confidence that I wasn't going to drink too much. He kept his eyes on the computer screen: You get very maudlin when you're drunk. It was clear from his posture that he was reliving some unsavoury flashback and trying to disguise the discomfort he felt in the presence of an overly emotional attention-seeking daughter. I pocketed my phone, keys, wallet, and fled onto the

Cleaner

street. My entire life seemed to be taking place on the streets of late, always trying to get somewhere with either the sun or the moon judging above me. Why was everything always the same? Massive ego; low self-esteem. It seemed too early in the morning to cry. In town, I became drawn to the sound of people and music and hoped it was some kind of street festival I could lose myself in. However, when I got closer, it became clear it was a protest and a counterprotest about trans rights: over a boombox blasting mariachi music, a disgruntled woman with glasses could be seen mouthing the word 'penis' to the chagrin of the anti-TERF crowd. I went and hid in the library instead, to recuperate amongst the safety of colourful bookshelves and take an early siesta on a beanbag chair. In the afternoon Paul rang me to say he was on his way with the van. Having all of a sudden run out of time, I splashed out on an Uber to the gallery. My driver seemed lonely; we spoke at length about his pet hawk and how he takes it hunting in the forest catching wood pigeons, not ghetto pigeons. Pedigree. We spoke for a while about keeping birds — how my grandad used to keep lost pigeons in a purpose-built shed at the bottom of the garden. How he'd quietly mess with them in the evenings and drive my grandma nuts. Those infinite Sundays I'd help him feed them all singing 'tuppence a bag'. When we arrived at the gallery, the Uber driver wouldn't unlock the doors until I'd appraised three photos of his hawk. To his credit, it was rather beautiful and I told him so. He smiled and smiled. After all that faff, I ended up beating Paul to the venue. I was determined to be unbothered, so I strained against the brickwork for a relaxed posture. He pulled up a couple of minutes later in sunglasses and a new haircut. Hey. There was no time to have sex or make him lunch: we got straight to work hauling the canvases out of the van so the driver could go to his next gig. Paul ran his fingers through his new hair: The venue looks good! What time does the owner get here? As if he had summoned her, she pulled up in her Fiat 500 and shook both our hands warmly with her stick arms. Lovely, whiny posh girl. There was no recollection in her eyes, which was more hurtful than I'd expected: So glad you've chosen us to represent you! After she unlocked the door, I was led inside to sign a few things at her desk while Paul made a start carrying the paintings inside. The floor was dustier than I wanted it: Shall I vacuum this for you? Posh Girl looked at me askance: Don't worry, I'll get the cleaner to do that for us when she gets here. Oh, right. I began setting up and curating the space, bullying Paul into rearranging everything tenfold until the vein on his forehead reminded me of a tree root. Overall, I was happy with the composition and felt that if the punters looked at my work in the order I designed, they would feel the full effect of the experience. My plan was set. There was just enough time before the grand opening for Paul and me to eat takeaway sushi on the dusty floor of the gallery and reminisce. Through the shop window, the sunset washed over us in a great horizontal line, as if we were in a space shuttle on the very edge of the solar system. It was calm, nice. I went to the disabled toilet to sit on the lid for a moment of quiet reflection and was rewarded with the sight of my first grey hair in the mirror, shining forth as a harbinger of change. The scene was different when I returned: Posh Girl was ripping into an androgynous figure standing with a hanging head by the door. She was too late to start cleaning the place now, the exhibition was going to start any minute — she should have been here on time like she was asked! The figure shrugged involuntarily, scarecrow-like, moving to put away the Henry Hoover she'd yanked out of the cupboard. Wait! Please! (I spoke in a voice that felt no longer my own.) Please… do your job while the exhibition goes ahead. Clean! The three of them stared at me like I was insane. The cleaner spoke to me for the first time in a pointy voice: You want me to clean during the thing? Yes, I said, it's perfect — let's pop the prosecco! And so the exhibition officially opened to the rumble of the vacuum. Paul cued up some ambient classics on Spotify and we waited for the hordes to arrive, not that there were many hordes to speak of. After a while, it became clear the most lucrative strategy was for Paul to stand in the street and shepherd people in with his charm and male charisma. FREE PROSECCO AND FREE ART! Once a steady current began to take shape, I stationed myself by the donation box to paint and sketch the composition: the students mid-pub-crawl, the sincere German tourists, the retired headteacher and her grandson, my parents and Tatiana, the confused but enthused hen party.

Cleaner

Some left immediately, some stayed longer to drink. Posh girl really came into her own in her little Zara blazer and got people networking in a way I couldn't fully register, even as I watched her do it. My mother of all people befriended the hen of the hen party; she and her coop were bedecked in crowns made of penises of all shapes and sizes arranged in wonky crenels. The hen's eyes were big and sparkly: This is amazing, thank you for having us! We love a bit of culture, you know, despite what FUCKING STEVE thinks (the bridesmaids whooped in unison). Nah, I love him really... your mum must be so proud of you for doing all this! I turned to my mother: Are you proud of me? She was ambivalent: I don't know, darling, do you think I'm proud of you? I don't know. Well, it's what you think that matters most (she twisted her body away, towards the next canvas) so... what's happening in this one? She pointed to the painting of The Erotica Man and me meeting in the bar, the words salvaged from his crappy erotica swirling round us in an elusive, abstract jumble. In a moment of uncharacteristic honesty, I told her the truth and she listened, brow furrowed: So you think your art is fixing his art? The candour of her question caught me off guard. I guess so, maybe not fixing, more… uplifting. She laughed heartily and said it was that school trip all over again. What school trip? When you were supposed to go to that Tudor mansion but you were sick so I kept you off, do you remember? And the next day you were supposed to design a poster for the mansion but obviously you didn't go, so you decided that you'd help that bratty-bitch-cow that sat next to you, fixing her work — you know, the one that kept giving you nits and had the really slutty communion dress, the one that hated you even though you were obsessed with her. You must remember her! I had to go into school for a meeting about it because they were concerned. Anyway, the teacher was so impressed she gave bratty-bitch-cow a prize, even though you'd done it for her. And you came home and told me all about it, all upset, as if the teacher was supposed to magically know it was your work. My mother took a sharp breath in: You've always had a bit of a martyr complex — oh, don't look at me like that, it was a joke! I didn't get to reply because, to the surprise of everyone, my brother and Des Moines arrived in matching pale pink hoodies and gnomish smiles. Hello. Hi. Didn't expect to see you both, how are you? Fine thanks. While my mother hugged Des Moines, my brother nudged me on the shoulder and told me this thing 'wasn't as shit as he was expecting', Des Moines whispered that I was 'very talented', flashing a small sapphire gaze into mine. In the black hole of her pupil I only saw the pit of her for a moment before she slipped back into quiet small-talk: This place is so cool, I'm loving the body-positivity vibes! Muted and poignant, Des Moines had finally become an appropriate match for my regular English brother. They wandered about the exhibits as a unit, holding hands fiercely, their backs to people as they examined one painting after another. Leaving them be, I floated to the corner of the room where my father was speaking with an enormous punk with a thinning mullet about Piaget. When I joined them The Mullet Man appraised me: This is your daughter, the artist? Some of this is good (he pointed to the nude Isabella had drawn of me, now framed. I hadn't claimed it as my own per se, but rather put it centre stage as part of my summoning-Isabella plan). Prosecco wetted the corner of Mullet's impressive moustache: I have a question — I always ask this, he said — where do you get your inspiration? We all chuckled blithely at such a clichéd question and I explained, coolly, as if I was just thinking about this truth for the first time, that sometimes I get so anxious about not doing anything that I either paint everything or nothing at all. Thinning Mullet shrugged his moustache in appreciation. My father, on the other hand, nodded slowly at this assessment of my character, budding his mouth open to say, simply: My daughter was born on a slippery slope. The men laughed heartily, all teeth and skull, and the headless nude of me seemed to laugh on the paper, and so I practised laughing with them, holding up my palms in a modest 'time to mingle' pose. I couldn't take any more. When they'd turned their backs on me, I took the nude and hid in the disabled toilet with a half-bottle of prosecco snatched from under the awning of the plastic leafy selfie station. In the toilet, I propped the nude against the wall and drained the bottle in one maudlin gulp. Burped. Looked in the mirror at myself and considered whether I was proud of my slippery slope. Needing more reassurance, I rooted through my scalp to find the grey hair from earlier but for some reason it wasn't where I'd left it. I scrabbled and pulled my head around to no avail and was left wondering, not for the first time, if I had hallucinated the symbol. I sat down heavily on the toilet seat. What had I done wrong? Some part of it had not yet manifested, some thread in the tapestry remained unwoven. I felt so sure she would come. What had I missed? The cyclical structure shape had been adhered to, I'd taken myself right back to the start at the gallery where we had met and I'd emerged from the chrysalis as an artist like I had needed to. This was my exhibition. I was here as an artist. Or at least, I came across like an artist. That was the main thing. What else did I need to do to summon her properly? What part of the ritual had I neglected? I'd even put her drawing centre stage of my exhibition because I was an artistic martyr, the best martyr, the most loyal martyr the world had ever seen. I positioned the sketch on the toilet seat where it had been before and knelt in front of it, looming over myself like sad God again, wishing I had the thin white line of cocaine trailing up the pencil line of my hip to complete the mimicry of our first meeting. Maybe the blankness she'd left on the sketch where my face should have been was because she never wanted to see me after all. I curled downwards in prayer or pain or something, looking at this sketch because I still didn't know what it meant that she drew me like this, and without thinking I pressed my nostril to the paper, breathed in nothing... Then it happened: she barged in through the door, busting the lock (of course she had to break the lock!) and looked at me. Not Isabella. The cleaner. It was the cleaner, because of course it was supposed to happen this way. The cleaner had barged in on me in the bathroom like she was supposed to, to see the image of the artist crouched over the toilet seat, over her own drawing. Ohmygod, sorry, I didn't mean to — I knew exactly what to say: You're not going to tell on me, are you? What? I repeated: You're not going to tell on me, are you? What? Just tell me you're not going to tell on me, I said. The look in her eye was nothing less than oceanic: I'm not going to tell on you? I grinned at her; and the cycle was complete. I stood up slowly (oh God, so slowly) and approached her step by step until we were facing each other, toe to toe and face to face and my hand was twining upwards to cup

Cleaner

her cheek. I leaned in with a kissing mouth full of destiny and time but tasted hell— I didn't see the Domestos power-foam spray bottle (Arctic fresh) in her hand. She retreated back towards the door: What the fuck is wrong with you? I spat the toilet cleaner into the sink, rinsed my mouth out. When I looked up again, she was still there, apparently waiting for an answer, despite the fact her question seemed rhetorical. What the fuck is wrong with you? I looked at the cleaner, the reflection of her in the bathroom mirror, and said either: 'I forgive you' or 'I'm proud of you'— one of them, I can't remember. Then I walked out, out of the bathroom and straight back into the exhibition. Re-entering the space felt like puncturing a bubble; a stony crowd was gathering at the far end of the gallery around something I couldn't see. This was my exhibition: What's going on? Thick voices were hissing urgently in rapid quickfire. Something about 'turning up like this' and 'really appreciate it if you would leave'. A bitchy, unmistakable voice from the centre of the crowd: But I was invited? My stomach lurched magnetically. I pushed my way through the scrum to look at her and see if she was real. It's impossible to say how long I stared at her. Whenever I read books where a character comes back after a long time, the narrator always seems to notice their eyes first or something before they see the dramatic change. I find it unrealistic. Anyway, her swollen, pregnant belly straining from underneath her T-shirt naturally caught my attention first. Then I looked into her eyes. They were freezing: Hi _____. Hello, Isabella. (Lightning.) She licked her lips: So where's my drawing then? It's in the bathroom, I said. Whiny Posh Girl chimed in, squaring her Zara blazer shoulders: No, you're not going in my bathroom again, not after last time! Isabella grinned at me and Whiny Posh Girl looked at me with stunned, delayed recognition. My mother jumped in, in manager mode: As I was saying, we'd really appreciate it if you'd leave... She trailed off, trying not to look at Des Moines in the corner with my brother, quietly exploding. Naturally all she could look at was Isabella's belly. It was all any of us that were in her orbit, however vaguely, could do. Illogical as it was, it really felt like Isabella had murdered Des Moines' baby with the cursed gender-reveal portrait, stolen the baby parts, unravelled them from Des Moines' womb with her own hands, and knitted them somehow into her own. I wouldn't have put it past Isabella. Murder is an art, after all. And looking into Des Moines' pink, crumpled face, I knew it was exactly what she was thinking too. She grabbed at my brother and hissed: Get her out of here! Isabella, impassive: But I was invited! The only person who seemed neutral was Paul, calmly washing up glasses in the mini-sink, sponge in hand. Was he calm because he knew or because he didn't want to know? Despite the emotional chaos of the scene, I didn't feel so overwhelmed. When the curt, clipped requests turned into shouting and screaming and 'I am the owner of this establishment' and 'I was invited to this fucking thing, my art is on display!' and 'call yourself an artist after that gender-reveal shambles!' and 'shagging her in my bathroom last year!' and 'charged us a small fortune for that painting!' and 'how do you know _____ anyway?' I was intoxicated with it all. All these people were here because of me, I'd made this happen — this was the real art. When the shouting turned into middle-class English/American pushing and shoving and 'Don't push me, I'm fucking pregnant, you bitch' and 'Don't touch *me*, I've just had a stillbirth, you cunt', Tatiana tugged at my sleeve: Who is woman with the… ? (she mimed the shape of pregnancy with her hands). I smiled lightly and told her the truth: I don't know. When talks about calling the police started and the broom came out to sweep the shattered glass, I made my move; hooking Isabella's elbow and dragging her onto the street huffing and puffing. Where are we going? I don't know, where do you want to go? I don't know! We ended up sitting in an empty bus shelter at the top of the high street, while Isabella caught her breath in angry, cloudy gasps. The smell of chips wafting from the chip shop didn't seem to match the drama of the situation and her hand resting on her distended stomach was so freakishly normal I wanted to paint it there and then. How long have you been back? (She didn't answer.) Why did you invite me? (I didn't answer.) Why did you come? (Mean pause.) Because I was bored. Oh. We couldn't speak then because the bus arrived, heavy and elephantine, and the sound of it cushioned the fall of all my delusions. We sat there, the passengers alighted, and the bus left and the street was quiet again. Isabella sighed: I was bored… and my art was supposed to be on display in a real exhibition, so I thought I'd come and see it. I looked at her and, in her expression, saw something like yearning, something like disappointment. She was real. She looked down at her stomach, disappearing again. Do you want to see a picture of the ultrasound? She got out her phone and scrolled through what felt like a hundred images of the foetus: I had to get the 3D ultrasound done like four times because the baby just wasn't cooperating and giving me a good angle. This is the best one, look (she held up a yellowy picture of a mournful little face) but the fucking umbilical cord is in the way and, I don't know, it's just throwing the composition all off. She handed me her phone for a closer look while she rambled on about gender reveals and birth plans and babymoons and gentle parenting and nesting. The more I looked at this foetus on the screen the more its face fell, as if it knew it was being sculpted and projected beyond itself; futuristic and regressive at the same time, like it had already been suffocated and preserved in a bog like the Tollund man, before it had the chance to be new. I looked from the screen to the bump and back again in freefall. Which one was the real baby? All I could see was a portrait.

An unhappy reality made itself known: if, before children can be themselves, they must be their parents' projects, then that means all parents are artists, for better and for worse. Some artists are better than others. I looked at Isabella and saw her properly, poised for glory and infatuated with her own artistry. Was she going to be a goalkeeper mum or be like my parents and goalkeep without hiding their disdain? Or perhaps something else? Isabella was still talking: I've spent so much money already, it's obscene, but I want a classic upbringing and, even though I hate social media, I'm thinking I'll try and go down the mumfluencer route because, you know, brand deals, but I already know for a fact I want to keep the baby tech-free because I'm not having an iPad kid, at least until I know that — she wittered on — hold on, is that a fucking egg? Distracted, Isabella pointed one of her long horrible fingers to a little concrete alcove next door to the bank. We got up to investigate and sure enough, it was an egg sitting next to maybe three or four matchstick twigs on the ground. Isabella: Why would someone leave an egg here? That's so weird. I told her that it was probably a pigeon egg. Isabella: Pigeons are so fucking pathetic. I shook my head: No, they're not. I mean they are, but it's not their fault; we domesticated them thousands of years ago and now they don't know what to do without us; we coddled them and then abandoned them. Isabella shrugged and clutched at her stomach: They're rats with wings that eat shit and shit everywhere and get in the way, look, they can't even build proper nests! I shook my head again: they don't know how. This is a stress egg. Something must've scared the pigeon away from its nest and this is likely the safest place it found — look, you can see she's tried to build a new nest but it was too late (the little round egg really did look pathetic on the dusty ground next to the flimsy twigs but, then again, the habitat is all wrong for it. Pigeons are never going to thrive here). It must have been desperate. Once she's laid, she's stuck and can't leave until it's hatched, but this egg is all alone... I looked up and, to my surprise, Isabella's face was all crumpled — for the first time in her life probably. I saw red: Don't pretend you give a fuck. She screwed up her face: I *don't*, it's the hormones. I stared down at the egg in its terrible nest, fighting visions of my boot crushing it out of its misery on the concrete floor, fighting the urge to deny it its inevitable mediocrity. It can't be anything other than what it is and maybe it's nobody's fault; the nature-nurture argument is kind of obsolete when the world changes too fast for your parents to know how to contain you. Isabella scowled and I wiped my eyes. *What are you going to do with yourself now then?* I stared down at the egg and the egg stared back up at me and then we both stared at Isabella's egg-belly and guts and wondered what she thought she was creating — Hey, she said, my eyes are up here. I kissed her very briefly because it felt like the right thing to do. Her lips, cheek and tongue were feather-soft. She kissed me like life was only about having fun and feeling good and I kissed her back like I was just having fun and feeling good. Then her bus came and she got on it without a word. We waved goodbye to each other through the smeared window and she was gone. I turned back to the egg. The little white black hole. The little doomed pearl of failure like me. I knew, rather than felt, that the pigeon had done the best it could to build a nest, even if it wasn't enough — deep down, even I knew that pity for pigeon-parents is not unwarranted. They were

Cleaner

doomed to fail too and their best is never enough. Baptised in my own tears, I felt meaningless, I felt reborn. It was time to go. The street was empty and the egg was fucked. Still. I stripped off my jumper and T-shirt, shivered back into my jumper and scooped the egg into a makeshift fabric nest. I looked for a little tree with supportive branches and found one not too far from my parents' house. I placed it as high as I could. I did my best.

Acknowledgements

I've been the recipient of extraordinary kindness throughout the process of writing and publishing *Cleaner*.

Edwina de Charnacé, my agent; forever in awe of your tenacity, energy and your know-how. Thank you for choosing me. Thank you, Jo Dingley, my editor, for smart, gentle, thoughtful commentary and nudging me into the story I totally planned to tell all along. So grateful to everyone at Bedford Square, particularly Claudia Bullmore, Polly Halsey and Jamie Hodder-Williams for taking a chance on a weird book and inviting me into the world of publishing with care.

I'm also so grateful to staff on the Warwick Writing Program. Thanks in particular to Ian Sansom for magic teaching and Gonzalo C. Garcia for patience, invaluable guidance and encouragement as *Cleaner* was engendered. Thanks to Iosi

Havilio (who has absolutely no idea who I am) for writing a lightning book called *Petite Fleur* that *Cleaner* would not exist without. And thank you to my peers on the MA in 2020–2021 for community and criticism including but not limited to; Phil Melanson, Chandler Coniglio, Yasmin Inkersole, Nina Kenney, Jaan Sõmermaa, Carlotta Ottonello.

Finally, it goes without saying but I'm infinitely grateful for the love of my family and I'm infinitely grateful to each and every one of my friends for their love. It's lovely to be loved; I'm rescued in it, made better in it. I'm so lucky to have more names to mention than can fit my word limit; Abi Cody, Matt Smith, Lizzie Mclurgh, Francesca Hyde, Katie Burke, Joanna Burke. My Crescent family; Rob Laird, Beth Gilbert, Tom Lowde, Amanda Nickless, Poppy Starling, Jordan Starling, Chloe Potter, James Tandy, Charlotte Thompson, Vicky Youster, Luke Plimmer, James Knapp, Steve Davis, Fi Cotton, Grace Cheatle et al. Special mention for Andrew Cowie for lovingly picking out my typos and, of course, Andrew Elkington for reading *Cleaner* first. It had to be you x

About the Author

Image © Beth Gilbert

Jess Shannon was born and raised in Birmingham. She is a proud graduate of the University of Warwick Writing Programme, completing her degree in Literature and Writing in 2020 and her Masters in Writing in 2021. She lives and works in Solihull and hates cleaning.

Bedford Square Publishers is an independent publisher of fiction and non-fiction, founded in 2022 in the historic streets of Bedford Square London and the sea mist shrouded green of Bedford Square Brighton.

Our goal is to discover irresistible stories and voices that illuminate our world.

We are passionate about connecting our authors to readers across the globe and our independence allows us to do this in original and nimble ways.

The team at Bedford Square Publishers has years of experience and we aim to use that knowledge and creative insight, alongside evolving technology, to reach the right readers for our books. From the ones who read a lot, to the ones who don't consider themselves readers, we aim to find those who will love our books and talk about them as much as we do.

We are hunting for vital new voices from all backgrounds – with books that take the reader to new places and transform perceptions of the world we live in.

Follow us on social media for the latest Bedford Square Publishers news.

@bedsqpublishers
facebook.com/bedfordsq.publishers/
@bedfordsq.publishers

https://bedfordsquarepublishers.co.uk/